I0708887

ISBN- 978-1-7384046-4-3

Cover Art and Book Design by Emma Russell
"The End" Illustration by Jay Nyx

More by Emma Russell:

Welcome to Wonderland
By Order of Chaos

Coming Soon:

The Flintlock Pistol and the Silver Bullet
The Diary of Lilith Drayke

Main Character Pronouns:
Bellerose- She/Her
Adeline- She/Her
Wilmot- He/Him
Caris- She/Her
Alvis- They/Them
The Spirit- They/Them

Beauty and Beast

*To anyone who wishes they had this kind of fairytale
growing up.*

Proglogue

Adeline Stone's tenth birthday was a disaster. Not because of any wrongdoing on her part. This was not some whiny bratty child crying a storm because the cake was the wrong shape or there were an odd number of presents.

No, in the case of Adeline Stone, it was her parents who got everything wrong. As it turns out, her family were royalty by corruption only. Barely two moments after Adeline was born, her mother and father made a deal. A deal with the dark spirits of their world, a deal that would ultimately be their downfall.

Royalty. Life eternally in comfort and riches. Power over the common people of the land. All in exchange for a price. A price to be paid in ten years.

But ten years? Surely ten years was enough time to reap the rewards of the opportunity they had exploited. Ten years to pay one silly little price.

A silly little price paid on Adeline Stone's tenth birthday.
The dark spirit returned, cloaked in darkness, twisting ram-shaped horns protruding from vine-like hair. Eyes wide and white, devoid of life. A ghostly shape entered the ballroom and put out all light. The guests of Adeline Stone's tenth birthday party fled.

Adeline's father fell to his knees before the spirit. Adeline's mother pushed her daughter behind her.

"Spirit," Her father's voice trembled as he put his hands together. "Please, we ask for more time."

"Time?" The spirit cackled. "You have had plenty of it. I was generous by offering you a decade."

Her father bowed his head. "Yes, yes, we know Spirit. Please, our daughter-,"

"Ah, yes. Your daughter." The spirit pointed a long twig-shaped finger to Adeline's mother. "Bring her here."

Her mother held onto Adeline. "What do you want with our daughter?"

The spirit's smile was wicked. "She is the price."

Her parents froze in place. Her mother's nails were digging into Adeline's arm. Slowly, her father got to her feet. "My daughter, she is the price we must pay?"

"Yes, unless you want to pay it instead?"

At that moment, Adeline's heart broke. Her mother, with no pause or ceremony, no pleas to the spirit, shoved Adeline forward. Adeline fell before the spirit, whose smile turned to a low and deep frown.

"You do not wish to fight for her? Fight for the miracle you have been given?"

"If that is the price." Her mother stated, standing up a little straighter. "Then let it be paid. As long as we can keep what we worked so hard for."

"Worked? Worked?!" The spirit howled with laughter, throwing their head back, a hand on their chest. "Only cowards seek me out. And only cowards would let the innocent take the blame."

The spirit leaned down to Adeline, floating in the air, and gripped Adeline's shoulder with a tight hand. Vines, covered in thick ivy leaves, curved around Adeline's neck and hair, tightening on her forehead and throat.

Adeline Stone screamed, and when the ivy released her, her parents screamed too.

For Adeline Stone was no longer a ten-year-old girl. But a ten-year-old beast. Two, great mighty horns grew out from her hair, twisted like the trunk of an oak tree. Her ears were pointed, much like the forest spirits in the stories she had read. Her cheekbones were raised, puffing out of her skin, and her nose had widened. She resembled an animal, a deer or goat, or something in between. Her whole body had changed. Her hands felt stiff, with sharp claws. Her legs were shaped like a mighty stag, but they were covered in tree bark, as was the rest of her skin. Adeline screamed, her pink dress ripped to shreds around her.

Her mother's voice cracked from the scream she let out. "What have you done?!"

Her father charged past Adeline, and towards the spirit. "Change her back. Change her back. She can't be seen like this!"

The spirit started to fade away. "The price is paid. For now."

Adeline, in her new body, felt a coldness deep in the core of her soul. Her now yellow eyes glanced over to her parents, who stood, staring at what was in front of them.

"Mother?" Adeline called out, in a low voice that did not sound like her own.

Her mother put her to bed that night. Her father wished her a pleasant sleep. When they tucked her in, there was a look in their eyes. At the time, Addy did not know how to describe it. But it was disgust.

The next day, they were gone. And so were the servants and workers of the castle.

It was empty. Except for the beastly child known as Adeline Stone, whose tenth birthday party had been a disaster.
Adeline checked every corner of the castle. It was difficult, she was adjusting to her new weight, her new legs. She hugged the walls and shuffled down every hallway. She even tried checking the tunnels that ran under the castle, but they were empty, and the exits into the forest were sealed off. Everyone was gone. There was nothing left. Nobody left.

Eventually, Adeline stumbled into the ballroom. It was still full of the remains of the party. Unopened presents, a cake that was now going stale. And in the middle of the ballroom, to this child's surprise, was the dark spirit that had cursed her.

Adeline tried to will herself to move, but the fear grounded her to remain still. The spirit moved closer, malicious in their movements. But they did not cause more pain and only knelt before Adeline, and lifted a rough hand to her face.

"I am sorry my child." They said, voice soft with remorse. "I am sorry you had to pay the price for this debt."

"But why me?" Adeline's words were quiet, as she held back the tears. "Why did you have me pay the debt?"

The spirit's sigh was heavy and sent a cold breeze through the room. "Because I knew they wouldn't pay it. And I thought they would have enough love for you to volunteer themselves."

Adeline bit back a sob and her voice trembled. "You didn't have to ask for payment. You didn't have to say there was a debt..."

"Adeline." The spirit moved to hold her hands in their new form. "Anyone who makes a deal with the spirits must be ready to pay the debt. It is how it must be, or there is a great imbalance. Your parents knew what they were doing, and they were too scared to pay the price."

"Is it bad that I'm not angry at them for running away?"

The spirit shook their head, pulling Adeline closer and putting its arms around her. "Not at all, my child."

Adeline rested her head on the spirit's shoulder, the two sets of horns knocking against each other. The spirit chuckled. "I will help you if you wish it."

She lifted her head, meeting the spirit's eyes. "Can you get my parents to come back to pay the debts?"

The spirit's white eyes narrowed. "How did you know there was more to pay?"

"Yesterday you said the price was paid, for now. How many deals did they make with you?"

"Many deals, and with many deals come many debts. But only your parents can pay those prices. However, your current state is not permanent. It is only a curse. And though I cannot reverse it entirely, I can mitigate its effects."

"How?"

The spirit took one of Adeline's hands again. There was a softness to the dark spirit, a different demeanour to what it was yesterday. "Let us make a deal."

Adeline took a step back, letting go of the spirit's hand. "No, no deals. Please, I want no debts."

"Relax my child, and hear what I must say. All I ask is that you stay here at the castle. By doing that, I will allow you to pay a debt your parents left."

Adeline frowned, thinking for a long time. "But, I cannot stay here by myself. I am still a child."

The spirit chuckled. "I may be a dark spirit, but I am not a cruel one. I will make it so you will be taken care of. Nobody will remember that your parents, or you, were royalty, and you will not be bothered while you grow up. This castle, you see, is enchanted. Always was, ever since your parents first got it. It can cater to your every need, and better yet, I will ask the spirits here to watch over you, and guide you."

Adeline jumped in surprise. "There are spirits here?"

The spirit's smile grew wide. "There always have been, you have simply never been able to see them. Now, Adeline, do you understand this deal and this debt?"

She nodded, as her hands shook. "Yes, but why are you doing this for me?"

The spirit took her hands once more to stop them from trembling. "I want to give you a chance, my child. One your parents would have never given you."

Adeline thought back to yesterday, to how she was thrown before the spirit. She wondered, in the back of her mind, whether her parents knew she would be the price, and would have her pay it all along.

The spirit held her hands gently. "There is one final thing. This castle taking care of you is out of kindness. However, there is still an exchange, a debt. Your remaining here is how you pay the debt to it. But if you extend this kindness to anyone else, they will have to pay a price. Do you understand?"

"Yes." Adeline's voice was firm. "I understand. What must I do to break my curse?"

The spirit's smile was sad. "You sound determined. I forget, under this appearance, that you are still only a girl. But no matter."

Vines grew outwards from the dark spirit's body, encasing itself and Adeline. Soft, wisp-like flames appeared inside the cocoon of trailing ivy, illuminating the darkness inside.
Adeline swallowed her fear as the spirit spoke. Their voice was as hard as wood and echoed.

"To love is to love without condition, without reason or rhyme.
What that is you must seek to define.
Find love where love could not be found,
Let the love be natural and let it be profound.

The ivy vanished, and the spirit remained holding Adeline's hands. The young Adeline was unsure of what any of it meant.

"I have to find love?" Adeline asked, trying to understand the words spoken to her.

"Yes. However long it takes, you must find it."

"But..." The tears started to run down Adeline's face. "I cannot leave. How can I find love?"

The spirit lifted a hand and wiped the tears away. "I cannot tell you how, or when. But know this curse is not impossible to break. All I ask is that you keep this determination with you, and remember to always have kindness in your heart. Can you do that for me, Adeline?"

She nodded, and the spirit opened their arms. Adeline fell into the embrace, sobbing into the spirit's hollow chest. The dark spirit began to fade, disappearing into a dwindling light.

"I believe in you." The spirit said as they vanished.

Adeline was on her knees in the middle of the ballroom. She swallowed the lump in her throat, and wiped her tears, trying to bring herself to her feet. But her new legs were still shaky, and hard to walk with. She fell back to the ground.

Then a soft feminine voice called out from behind her. "Oh dear, now we can't be having this can we?"

Adeline used her hands to turn herself around, turning to face the voice. Her eyes widened, as she stared into a womanly face, with flowing and floating white hair. Her eyes were white, like the dark spirit's. But she walked with heavenly grace and human mannerisms.

"Are you one of the castle spirits?" Adeline asked, trying again to get to her feet.

"Indeed I am, my dear. It is wonderful you can see me. Here, let me help you up." The spirit walked towards her and offered both hands. Adeline took them and was pulled to her feet.

"Who are you?"

The spirit smiled wide. "I'm Caris. You are Adeline, yes? Do you prefer that name, or perhaps would you like to be called Addy?"

Adeline thought for a moment. "I like Addy."

Caris put an arm around Addy, supporting her as she walked. "It is a beautiful name. Now, why don't we get you something to eat? You can meet everyone else."

"There are more of you?!" Addy exclaimed, a surprise in her voice as she put a hand on the ballroom door.

Caris laughed. "Yes, plenty more. We will take care of you, I promise."

As time passed, Addy become more and more acquainted with the spirits that had promised to look after her.

Caris was the mother Addy had lost.

Wilmot taught Addy how to walk again, and how to stand tall with power and grace.

Alvis helped her search the castle library and imparted all of their knowledge to her.

There were other spirits, who drifted in and out of Addy's life, always coming back to tell her the stories of their adventures, to impart a moral lesson to her. Always a reminder to be a better person than her parents were. And always, *always* to pay her debts.

A decade passed without warning. The spirits were overjoyed to see Addy grow into a mature young woman. Under the bestial form, which had grown with her, they found a woman with a good heart and a curious mind.
Even as the castle fell into disrepair, it continued to take care of her. Ivy continued to grow, and the trees grew wide, creating a forest within the castle walls. One day, in an unusually selfish request, Addy asked for a little colour among all the green, and the castle gave her a rose garden near the stone fountain. Most of the stones outside were cracked, the outside walls breaking under the strain of the ivy. But the castle held strong, ready for the day Addy broke the curse.

But Addy knew that day would never come. One night, by the library fireplace, she told the spirits as such. Nobody remembered the castle existed, but there had been some visitors. Random people were arriving and asking for a night of shelter, thanking the mysterious master for their kindness. Sometimes, there would be raiders, looking for fortune, but they were quickly scared off.

Even so, Addy knew her fate. She wanted to believe in
the dark spirit's words, that someday it would happen,
but she was old enough and wise enough to know why
the dark spirit said such a thing.

It was kindness to a ten-year-old girl who had been
turned into a beast. Comfort and reassurance to make
them agree to one last chance of hope.

Caris was the leader in trying to encourage Addy to
continue hoping for a chance of happiness. Addy let her
down gently every time and continued on life as usual.

Hearing stories, learning lessons, all while losing hope.
All hope for love was lost. In the still nights, Addy
accepted that in this castle, she would rot.

Chapter 1

The Convenience of Marriage

Bellerose

The village of Reverie was small and quiet. Nestled in the middle of the roads that weaved around the forests, it was a humble farming village, content in its lack of desire for anything beyond the wheat fields and flour mills. Belle often pondered the idea of Reverie while on her walk to work. She always wondered what it would mean to search for more beyond the village borders. Everyone seemed content with staying right where they were, happy with a life of farming, marriage, and offspring. Rinse and repeat until they were all dried up. Belle's brothers often reminded her that life was that way. Her sisters enjoyed the part they played, a prize to be married off, with or without love.

Her father often told Belle to appreciate the simplicity she was blessed with. Appreciate the fact she never had to deal with complicated matters. Yet Belle had a yearning for more. Always more. She wondered if this was a flaw in her character, this greed that could never be satisfied.

Or this greed was something else entirely. Something she could not yet define.

She concluded her thoughts when she opened the front door to Reverie's modest library, which also doubled as the place where the village's administration was handled. She greeted the owner as she shut the door.

"Morning Mr Oliver, sir!"

Mr Oliver was facing one of the bookshelves when she entered and turned around with an eager spin to greet her as well. He smiled, running a hand through his long brown beard that reached his neck. He wore his everyday outfit, an off-white shirt, a dusted brown waistcoat, and a pair of trousers to match. It seemed his brown leather shoes were freshly polished.

"And what a fine morning it is Belle!"

Mr Oliver walked over as she put her satchel down behind the table and chair she called her desk. He placed a pile of books in her hands. "And perfect timing as well, these have just been returned to us by the Sunday school."

Belle inspected the covers, turning the books over in her hand. "Did the children enjoy them?"

Mr Oliver shrugged. "Who's to say? I don't concern myself with questions such as that. Put them back, if you could, and we can start going over the records that need updating."

The time passed, and soon the sun had reached its midday peak. Belle had sat behind her desk, fumbling through various sheets of paper and marking numbers with a small quill pen and a pot of ink. Her fingertips were stained black at this point as she checked the figures over and over again, passing them back and forth from Mr Oliver. Eventually, he declared they should take a five-minute break. He went into the back room, coming out a moment later with two mugs of warm tea, handing one to Belle before sitting back down. She thanked him with a smile and took a sip, the warmth filling her.

After a moment of silence, Mr Oliver turned to Belle. "Belle, may I ask you something?"

"Of course, sir." Belle put her cup down on the table, wiping her hands on the ends of her layered pastel blue skirt. "What is it?"

"I know you have been working for me for some time. I originally gave you this job because your father asked me so kindly. But there was another reason as well, it was so I could see what kind of woman you were, and whether you were going to be suitable for my boy Thomas."

Oh boy. Belle had hoped Thomas wouldn't be brought up.
Mr Oliver leaned forward in his chair, his hands clasped together. His sharp eyes pierced into Belle through his round glasses. "Did my boy do something to make you reject his proposal of marriage?"

It took a moment for Belle to process what she was hearing, for there were so many startling revelations at once. First, Mr Oliver only agreed to employ her to see if she was marriage material. Second, Thomas had told his father of Belle's rejection, when he agreed not to make a fuss. And finally third, that once again Belle could have nothing without a price to pay.

"It is nothing against him, Mr Oliver, please understand that." Belle fiddled with the hem of her skirt, avoiding his gaze. "Your son is a fine man."

"And he would make a fine husband. You two would do well together, so why turn down his offer?"

"He is not the right person for me Mr Oliver, but he would make a fine husband for somebody else."

Mr Oliver stood up turning his head to look at her before gathering the finished records. "Hm. And you're certain about that fact?"

Belle saw the look on his face, it was a face that lacked acceptance. But still, she wanted to stay firm on her decision. "Quite certain, sir."

"Perhaps you should take some time to think Belle. For if you do not wish to marry my Thomas, then there is no reason for you to continue to work here. And it would be a shame if I were to lose such a good worker over a matter such as this."

Her eyes widened, and Belle's jaw dropped open slightly. She stood up from her desk, striding towards him. "Sir, you can't be serious!"

Mr Oliver turned to face her. "I am. My boy needs a fine girl to make his wife and doesn't deserve anything less. Your father told me it was time for you to settle down. We agreed you would feel better if you had something to keep your head busy as well. Your income would appease you. Be grateful for the opportunity we have given you."

"So you're giving me an ultimatum. Marry Thomas, or lose this job."

And lose the freedom that came with it.

"Precisely." Mr Oliver nodded to her. "You are dismissed for the day. Go home and take some time to think about it. Let me know your decision in the morning."

Belle wanted to curse him under a thousand suns. In burning silence, she grabbed her satchel, and marched out, slamming the door behind her.

*****

Belle burst into the front room of her home and slammed the door shut behind her. Her two sisters, Mira and Clara, sat at the table in the centre of the room. The hearth, now nothing but dull embers, had burned out behind them. The two scowled as she came in, with Belle muttering curses under her breath as she took off her shoes and satchel, leaving them by the door.

Mira put down her teacup. "Oof, somebody's grumpy."

Clara did the same, crossing her arms. "Are you in a mood?"

Mira and Clara were Belle's sisters in blood only. She realised early on she had nothing in common with her two older sisters, who seemed to be cut from the same cloth, even though they were born a year apart. They matched only in appearance. Like Belle, they had beautiful dark brown hair that they wore in stylish braids and buns on their heads. The same chestnut brown eyes and elegant long eyelashes. Unlike Belle, however, who opted for a shorter and more practical dress, they wore lavish dresses with ruffled skirts above their ankles, with bodices that complimented their hourglass figures. Today, Mira's dress was a soft pastel yellow, and Clara's was a soft pastel pink. Both of them chose to wear a white ribbon in their hair.

Belle turned to them and put her hands on the table, staring them down. She knew her sisters were the busiest busybodies in town, and knew everyone's business. "Did you know Thomas told his father I rejected him?"

Mira put a hand to her chest and gasped. "You rejected Thomas?! What would you do that for?"

Belle raised an eyebrow, confused by the extreme reaction. "Because I didn't want to marry him?"

"Why not?" Clara asked, chiming in. "He's a handsome lad."

"Answer the question." Belle snapped back, rolling her eyes. "Did you know about it?"

"Well," Mira smirked. "We did overhear him telling Eder and Faron that he needed to be honest with his father about something. We couldn't work out what that was."

"Until now," Clara added.

Mira's smirk grew wider. "Father is going to be so upset with you."

Belle slumped into the chair, putting her face in her hands. Of course, her brothers were friends with Thomas. She had a feeling they would have encouraged him to tell his father everything.

Clara leaned over and put a hand on Belle's shoulder, moving her chair closer to do so. "You need to stop rejecting everyone Belle, or you're going to end up a spinster."

"I've already told you, Clara, I'm not ready to get married. Especially not to somebody I don't love."

Mira shook her head. "Is it because you're not ready to be married or you haven't found someone to meet your ridiculously high standards?"

"What are you talking about?" Belle asked, though she already knew what point her sisters were trying to make.

"You know exactly what Mira is saying," Clara stated with her eyes rolling. "Belle, whatever it is you're looking for, you're not going to find it."

"I'm not going to marry someone I would not be happy with."

"Happiness has nothing to do with it." Clara tapped her finger on the table. "You want perfection. Inside and out. You won't compromise."

Belle groaned. "What about your fiancees? I thought they were perfection. That's what you both said."

Mira had gotten engaged to Piero two months ago, and not long after, Adrian had proposed to Clara. Both were now in the throws of their wedding planning, and their latest topic of conversation often revolved around their bouquets and choice of music for the Reverie village band.

"Believe me, Piero isn't perfect," Mira said with a light chuckle, almost as if she was recalling all of her partner's flaws in one swift move. "But he is good, and kind."

"Exactly like Thomas is," Clara added, sighing. "Marry him, you could do worse."

The front door opened. As if right on cue, the two brothers, Eder and Faron, walked inside. They dropped their hunting equipment by the door, hanging their coats on the hooks, and kicked off their shoes, scattering mud over the floor.

"Spirits be damned, I have to clean that up, you know," Belle said with a scoff, leaning back into the wooden chair she sat on.

Belle's brothers, like her sisters, were a few years older than her but were twins. The two seemed to have inherited her father's physical traits, with their dirty blonde hair, but they shared the brown eyes that all of them did, something from their mother. The two wore their hunting gear, old green linen shirts, dirtied trousers and a leather belt. Eder sat down at the table, taking off his gloves. Faron followed him soon after.

"Why does Belle look like she's ready to explode?" Faron asked, putting his hands behind his head and relaxing into the chair. Belle coughed, choking in the air of mud and pinewood.

Mira let out a light laugh. "Since she's inevitably going to ask, did you two know Thomas told his father Belle rejected him?"

Eder's mouth turned into a gaping oval. "So that's what he was talking about the other day!"

Faron smacked his brother's arm. "It was obvious." He looked back to Belle. "I had a feeling you had turned him down. What, has something else happened?"

Belle put her head in her hands, sighing and looking at her brothers. "Mr Oliver said I would lose my job if I didn't accept his proposal."

Eder slammed a hand on the table, eyes wide with wild curiosity. "He said that?!"

Belle's sisters also looked shocked but remained sat at the table. Belle sighed, standing up, refusing to look at everyone's shocked looks of bewilderment. She went over to the hearth, relighting the fire and hanging the kettle over it. She gathered cups to make everyone tea.

From behind her, Mira's sharp voice cut through the silence. "For goodness sake, Belle, just marry him."

Belle looked over her shoulder to Mira. "No. I don't want to. And my job shouldn't be on the line over this."

Faron got up from his chair and walked over to Belle. He put a hand on her shoulder and turned her towards him. "You must have known that when Father got you that job it was so you could get to know Thomas. So when he proposed, it wouldn't be a surprise."

"Father never told me that. If I knew that was his and Mr Oliver's intentions, I would have never accepted it."

"Then why did you think you got to work there Belle?" Eder asked from the table.

Now Belle turned to face him. "I don't know, Eder. Maybe I thought I was smart enough to be employed on my own merits. I thought Father had seen how I loved the library and wanted to give me the chance to work there. But of course, I was naive."

She turned back to the stove. Faron stepped out of the way as Belle poured the hot water into the cups, and made everyone tea in silence. She put all their cups down and marched to where her brothers had dumped their muddy shoes, gathering them along with their coats.

"You're running out of time Belle," Eder said quietly.

Belle let out a sour chuckle, putting their things in a wicker basket. "And where is your wife, Eder? You too Faron, why haven't you found some lucky girl yet?"

Her brothers glanced at each other. Faron frowned. "Because we have more time than you."

Belle's shoulder slacked as she held the basket in her hands. She knew they were right. In the world they found themselves in, her brothers would always have more time than her. They were the glorious hunters who rode out every day to feed the village beyond grains and bread. They could have any girl they wanted, and any time they wanted. Nobody would say a thing if they turned down a proposal.

She frowned, biting her lip. "I'm going to go wash these off by the town well."

Faron nudged Eder, who stood up, dusting himself off and putting his shoes on. "We'll walk you there. We're meeting friends at the tavern."

"We'll come to meet you after you're done as well," Faron added, putting his shoes on and heading to the door. "We won't be too long."

Eder held out his hands to take the basket off her. Belle handed it to him with a smile and grabbed an empty wooden bucket with a scrubbing brush and soap already inside. Clara turned to Belle as the three of them walked to the door.

"Belle, could you wash yesterday's dresses as well?"

Belle sighed. "Not tonight. I can't wash your clothes together. These two have too much dirt and grime. Also...you can wash them yourself."

Mira groaned. "My hands are too delicate for such work."

"Then I'll wash them tomorrow." She turned to her brothers. "Let's go before it gets too dark."

The three of them walked out the door. As promised, Eder and Faron walked Belle straight to the town well as the afternoon sun still hung in their air, just before the evening fell. The large stone well stood in the centre of a circle of cobblestone paths. The town of Reverie had built stone benches around the well, and there were already splashes of water from when people had come by previously to wash their clothes. Eder even drew Belle a bucket of water, and the two of them left her to get to work, promising to be back in an hour.

The time passed as Belle sat there, back arched over and aching from scrubbing relentlessly at the stains her brothers had inflicted on their clothes throughout the day. She heard footsteps and looked up, thinking it was her brother's coming back. But instead, it was the last person she wanted to see today.

"Thomas." She said, trying not to let the anger slip through.

"Belle…" He replied in a sad tone. "Can I sit with you?"

She nodded. "I can't stop you."

He sat down next to her. She put down the scrubbing brush and wiped her hands on her skirt, noticing the ink and tea stains from earlier. She turned to him. There was no denying that Thomas was handsome. Hazelnut-coloured hair and sky-blue eyes. Sun-kissed skin and a strong physique from working as a farmer all day in the fields. Even as he sat in his dirty cloth overalls, he was pretty to look at. He could catch the eye of any girl he wanted. But Belle was not one of them.

He looked up at her, meeting her eyes, and started to speak. "I wanted to apologise on my father's behalf. I didn't know he was going to threaten your job with him."

"Why did you tell him?" Belle asked with a sigh. "You said you weren't going to raise a fuss about it."

"I wasn't going to, but I think he suspected something was wrong. Your brothers told me I should be honest with him. I promise I had nothing to do with how he reacted. I'm sorry Belle."

She smiled a little, turning her attention back to the clothes and boots that needed cleaning. "I appreciate the apology. Now if you'll excuse me Thomas I-,"

"Belle." His voice was soft.

She looked back up to him, and he reached for her hand, taking it in his own. Belle stiffened at his touch. "Would it be so bad if we were married?"

She found the courage to pull her hand away. "Thomas-,"

"I know it is not what you want but...you could still work at the library. I would never force you to do anything you didn't want to do. You would never have to have children or be...intimate. But we could be happy together, couldn't we?"

His look was soul-destroying. She slowly reached up to put a gentle hand on his arm. His expression froze as if he was trying to hold back tears. "Thomas, you are a good man. A kind, wonderful man. Exactly as your father says. And you deserve someone who can love you as you deserve to be loved. That person isn't me."

"It could be." He put his hand over hers. "With time."

Belle smiled at him. Knowing Thomas was speaking with genuine truth from his heart. "We would never have enough time. Time would pass, and we would come to regret it." She let her hand fall away. "You deserve a happy marriage. But it won't be with me."

Thomas lowered his head, and Belle could tell she had truly broken his heart. He swallowed hard, taking a few deep breaths before meeting Belle's eyes again. "Could we perhaps still be friends?"

She chuckled. "I don't see why not. Though your father has fired me for not accepting your proposal. But I'm sure we can overcome that hurdle with time."

He laughed with Belle. There was a sadness in his laughter, as he wiped his eyes and offered her a tight and warm hug, which she accepted. He stood up, apologising again for disturbing her. To show how sorry he was, he replaced her dirty water for her and then left.

Time passed again, and as promised, her brothers turned up exactly an hour after they left her. She was finishing wringing out their jackets when they turned up, smelling of the sharp sting of ale and rowdy sweat.

Faron took one look at Belle as Eder picked up the bucket and basket. He frowned. "You told him no, didn't you?"

Belle stood up, wiping her hands on her skirt once more. "Did you send him here?"

"I told him to give it one last chance. He didn't come back into the tavern looking the happiest."

She looked her brother in the eye, giving him a hard look. "I let him down easy. I was honest, I told him I didn't love him."

"You should have just said yes, Belle. You're lucky we're not cruel, and forcing you to marry some brute."

"Father promised me I could marry for love, exactly as Mira and Clara have. Don't start thinking you have any control over me Faron. I love you dearly brother, but this is my life. And these are my choices."

Eder stepped in between the two of them as Faron was about to reply. "Come on, the sun's setting. We don't want Father to be worrying about us, right?"

Faron sighed, his stern frown loosening. "I love you too, Belle. I only want you to have the best life you can."

"I know. Come on, Eder's right. We need to get home."

*****

Eder, Faron and Belle walked into the front door to find their father sitting at the table, putting various items of clothing into a cloth satchel. He looked up at the sound of the door, a bright smile on his face as he stepped forward to greet his sons.

"Boys! How are you both doing?" He asked, putting a firm hand on each of their shoulders. "How was the hunt?"

Belle's father was a stout and proud man. He was shorter than his sons and daughters but refused to let that stop him from being the main breadwinner of the household. very day he walked with pride. His thin white hair and curled moustache were always clean. He wore a beige shirt, brown coat and trousers, and tall leather boots. A merchant who commanded the finest ships, and walked the docks as master of his destiny.

"It went well, Father. How are the ships faring?" Eder asked, taking off his boots once more and scattering mud everywhere. Again. Belle tried not to sigh out loud.

"They do fine, my boy. Wonderfully fine." He patted Eder on the shoulder again. "And you Faron, how are you?"

"I am well Father." He replied, leaning down to embrace him.

Belle's father clapped his hands. "Excellent, excellent. Now, both of you get cleaned up."

Eder and Faron headed into their bedroom, shutting the door behind them. Belle could hear their chatter muffle. Finally, her father turned his attention to her. "Hello, my dear. How do you fare?"

Belle forced a smile. She hung up her brothers' coats back on the hooks to let them carry on drying and dropped their shoes underneath on the floor. Putting down the scrubbing brush and basket into the corner, she turned back to face her father.

"I fare well, Father. Considering today's events."

"Hm." Her father nodded, a roughness in his voice. "I heard from Mr Oliver. We'll discuss this after preparing dinner."

Belle looked towards one of the bedroom doors, the one she shared with her sisters. "Can Mira and Clara not assist us? Or Eder and Faron?"

"Your sisters have had a busy day as well, with their wedding announcements and preparations. And your brothers have been in the woods all day."

"I've been working too, Father."

"Yes, but your work does not demand much. Now come on, let us make a hearty stew with the meat your brothers brought home."

Belle shook her head but decided it was best not to argue. She began cutting vegetables and tossing them into the pot that her father had put on the stove. They worked in silence for a long while, until her father spoke.

"I did not think you would reject Thomas."

Belle didn't look up from cutting the vegetables. "I don't love him, Father."

"What's not to love? He is a good man, with a stable income. A kind family, honourable reputation." Her father explained as he sliced the meat. "He would be a wonderful husband if you gave him a chance."

"I would not want either of us to be in a loveless marriage. I told him as such. He understands."

"You are too stubborn," He replied with a chuckle. "You must get it from your mother."

The dead mother card. An underhanded move. Belle almost laughed at her father's attempts to change her mind. "You said I could marry for love."

Her father sighed. "I know I said that but I didn't think it would take this long. You could grow to love Thomas, perhaps it's something that takes time. You wanted that job so badly and now you're losing it because you won't take a good man's hand in marriage."

She started to drop the vegetables into the pot and grabbed a wooden spoon, stirring the bubbling liquid. "That job shouldn't have been based on whether or not I would marry. I don't appreciate being lied to Father."

"Belle, I never lied. I simply did what was best for you. You need to marry, like your sisters, and soon your brothers. I want nothing more than to see all my children happy."

"A marriage with Thomas would be unhappiness. Why do I need to marry at all?"

Her father put a hand on her arm. "Belle, look at me."

She looked up, lifting the spoon out of the pot. She met her father's cold brown eyes. "I have been kind to you, but the world is not as kind as me. You know what your place is in this world, and you must abide by it. Please, consider that." He took the spoon from her hand. "Go get cleaned up, I'll finish this."

Belle said nothing in response, and walked away from the stove, heading into her bedroom. Mira and Clara sat on their beds, stopping their giggling as Belle entered.

Mira crossed her arms. "So, he is upset."

"We said he would be," Clara added.

Belle tried not to get angry with her sisters again and turned to the side table, that had a bowl of water, a jug and a soft cloth. She washed her hands and face, getting the dirt and ink out from under her fingernails.

"Belle...you know we only say these things because we worry for you, right?" Clara said, standing up and walking over.

Belle used the cloth to wipe her face and hands dry. "There is nothing to worry about. I was perfectly content in my standing on what I wanted."

Mira turned herself around on the bed, turning to face Clara and Belle. "We don't always get what we want Belle. Sometimes, we get something we didn't expect."

She slammed the cloth down on the table and leaned against the wall. Belle ran a hand through her hair, fiddling with the ends. "But shouldn't I have control over that? It's my life."

Clara shook her head in defiance, putting a hand on Belle's arm. Her voice was firm, with no regret. "No, it's not."

Before Belle could respond, her father called them all for dinner. Sitting around the table was a morbid affair. However, delightful conversations about the current wedding plans had taken precedence over the current state of Belle's situation. Even her brothers mentioned in passing the women they were interested in. Her father promised he would find out more, eager to see her brothers find a loving wife to care for them.

After dinner, while Belle was cleaning the bowls and spoons, her father came out from his bedroom, wearing his hat and coat that he used for travelling. He was heading down to the docks again, as one of his ships was returning from overseas, and he needed to take stock. Eder and Faron loaded the carriage for him, and Belle prepared him some provisions to last him for the journey there and back. Mira and Clara sat at the table, another cup of tea in hand. Clara dabbed her eyes with a napkin, ever emotional about Father making a journey such as this.

Once he was fully packed, Belle's father bid goodbye to each of them with tight hugs and kisses on each cheek. He stood at the door, hands on his hips.

"Now, what would you like me to bring back for you?" He asked with a delightful smile.

This was always tradition. Every time their Father departed on a trip, he would bring them back something. No matter how tricky it was to find, he would find it. Belle never liked to admit it, but she loved the joy on her siblings' faces whenever he came back with exactly what they asked for. However, she was not sure if it was joy over the gift or their father's safe return.

"Clara and I have agreed we want a new lace shawl," Mira asked, sticking out her bottom lip and pouting. She put on a voice of a sickly sweet child. "One each."

"Absolutely my girls." He turned to Belle's brothers. "What do you want?"

"I want a new hunting knife," Eder said.

"I want a new bow," Faron added. "With arrows, please."

He had a proud smile on his face as he nodded to them. Finally, he turned to Belle, who stood at the back of the room, towards the kitchenette. "What do you want me to bring you back Belle?"

"I only want you to come home safely Father."

Her siblings groaned. Clara covered her forehead with her hand. "Ugh, not this nonsense again Belle. He always comes back."

Her father replied with a hearty chuckle. "You ask for the same thing every time. Let me at least get you something you can hold."

"Fine. A rose. They don't grow around here and I wish to have one to brighten up the dining table." Belle explained, flicking her wrist to the table her sisters sat at.

"My dear, I will get you a bouquet!" He said with a cheer and walked out the door waving goodbye.

Belle walked to the window, watching her father climb into the front of the cart, and grab the reins. The horse set off, pulling the cart and her father behind him, and she watched them both before they disappeared out of sight. She turned around, seeing her sisters already retire to their bedroom for the night. Her brothers bid her goodnight, and before she could protest, had shut the door.
They had left behind the mud on the floor, the cups on the table, and the ashes from the fire scattered in front of the hearth.

Belle sighed, burying her face in her hands. "So I'm the one cleaning this up I guess."

She grabbed the straw brush that was left leaning against the wall and opened the front door, sweeping out the debris of the day onto the front steps of the house. Once she had finished sweeping the steps as well, Belle sat down, her eyes naturally wandering up to the night sky.

She was trying hard not to think about tomorrow. When tomorrow came, she would not be able to wake up and go to the library. She would probably be forced out with her sisters, as they paraded around showing off their engagement rings. They would spend the day wandering in a strange bliss Belle could never comprehend.

But Belle wanted more. Maybe marriage would never be for her. She always thought one day she could be like her father, making grand trips to see what business had been brought in from the ships across the water.

Or maybe she could be on those ships herself.

Such dreams were not hers to dream. Some tomorrows were not destined to be hers.

Belle sat in the silence of the night. There were half as many stars as usual. In the distance, there were the sounds of joyful cheers from the tavern, of everyone making their way home to loving families and happy marriages.

Content. A feeling she would never know.

She curled up into herself, tightening her grip on her knees. The realisation set in.

In her stubborn rage, Belle had just ruined her life.

Chapter 2

It was a Dark and Stormy Night

Adeline

Addy reached up a long clawed hand to the curtain, being careful not to rip it as she pulled it back to watch the sky outside. She sat at the window, staring out into the darkness, watching the rain crush the land and the thunder crash into the ground. The forest stretched out beyond the castle walls, thick trees hiding the ground below.

Alvis stepped forward and grabbed the curtain from her, tucking it behind the curtain hook and standing next to her at the window. She turned to look at them, at the familiar face she had come to recognise as a member of her family. Alvis was almost see-through, translucent with a warm golden glow. They had no eyes, only hollow spheres that seemed to have a light of their own. But in other regards, Addy recognised the scholarly clothing, the collared shirt and rich robe with plenty of pockets. Although they were now ghostly white, Addy had an idea of what colours they would be wearing. Alvis told her often enough how fond they had been of wearing red.

"The storm seems to be quite furious tonight." She told them, noticing their gaze was drifting out the window as well. "I would not like to be outside right now."

"Aye, my dear. I pray for the souls who got caught in that. But let's hope they found shelter, eh?" They offered Addy a spectral hand. "Come on, the night grows weary. Caris does not want you to be up all night fretting."

Addy reached down and grabbed the book that was on her lap. Her claws tightened around the leather spine and cover. "I want to exchange this first. I finished it this afternoon."

Alvis chuckled, hand still outstretched. "My, my, dear. That seems to be a new record."

She took his hand and accepted the help to her feet. Despite ten years of cursed existence, her legs acted less human and more like the roots of a tree. Although they were shaped similar to a stag, she frequently lacked control over them. Her form was more vicious, and she lacked the delicacy a normal human body would provide her. It had taken years of practice to not ripe the walls or the books in the library.

Once she was standing, Addy walked over to the shelves. She remembered her lessons from Wilmot, to keep her back straight, head held high. To walk with purpose and stand dignified. She was not a monster inside, after all. Walking was an art she had gotten the hang of, but when she had sat for too long, her legs would sometimes refuse to collaborate.

Her hand tickled the spines on the shelves as she slotted the book back into its place. "It was a decent read, I suppose. A lot of talk of order and chaos, however."

"Chaos?" Alvis asked, drifting towards her.

"Yes, it's strange to read about fictional magic when we live in a reality with magic. It's a struggle to immerse yourself in something that is your truth."

"I can see what you mean." They replied, with a firm nod. "Do you want to be further carried into fiction, or would you prefer something founded in the world we live in?"

Addy thought for a moment, crossing her arms. She flinched at first, still forgetting the wooden texture that covered parts of her skin. The curse had grown with her. "Perhaps I could look through the botany books again? I still wish to identify some of the garden plant life."

"Of course Addy, let me-,"

The door to the library burst open, and Wilmot stood in the doorway, out of breath. He looked much like Alvis in his body, but Addy saw the shimmers of a knight's armour against his ghostly appearance. There was a worry locked on his face, the scar on his cheek creasing at his grimace.

"Your ma-," He cleared his throat. "Adeline. There seems to be someone approaching the castle."

Her head snapped up, and she stepped towards the door. "What do you mean? Nobody with a sane mind would be out in this storm."

"Those were my thoughts exactly. But a horse and cart are approaching the gates as we speak. I have eyes on them, but you best come see for yourself."

Addy tried not to sound too disgruntled by the inconvenience. She flexed her fingers and adjusted the dark green cloak she had hanging around her shoulders. "Alright Wil, let us take a look."

"I will come too, Addy," Alvis added, walking behind her as she followed Wilmot out the door.

The library was located on the second floor of the castle, facing the gardens and the never-ending forest. Wilmot, although aware Addy could not run fast, still hurried her towards one of the large front-facing windows.

"Right there, Adeline." He gestured outside, to the horse and cart now trudging along the smooth gravel path to the castle doors. "That's who I was speaking of."

Addy leaned into the glass, pressing her face against it to get a better look at the figure. To her surprise, it was an elderly-looking man. His face was frozen with fear, his clothes soaked. The cart was battered, with one wheel almost falling off. His horse looked as scared as he did, ready to run off at a moment's notice.

"The castle listens to you, Adeline." Wilmot continued. "You must decide what is best."

Addy lifted her face from the window, putting a hand to her forehead and furrowing her eyebrows as she thought. This was the first time in years they had someone approach the castle. The last lot was a band of hunters who were immediately thrown off by the copious amounts of potentially poisonous ivy that roamed the walls. She sighed through her teeth and looked up to Wilmot and Alvis, who were eagerly awaiting her decision.

"I have an idea. Alvis, find Caris, let her know what's going on and head for the main stairs. Wilmot, you and I will head to the stairs now."

"What are you thinking Adeline?" Wilmot asked.

"We are going to do what we always do. We are going to see who this man is, and we will show him kindness."

He nodded. "Alright. Alvis, we will meet you in a minute. Come, Adeline, let us wait for the doors to open."

*****

Caris and Alvis came rushing to the stairs once Addy and Wilmot had found a spot where they would not be seen. The central staircase, grand and wonderful, was the centrepiece of the castle entrance. Back when Addy was a child, it was where you could watch the many guests enter and exit the castle, where they would gape and awe at the splendour her parents had created. Now, it was decrepit and dusty. A grim reminder of all that had occurred.

"How far away is he from opening the doors?" Caris asked, sitting on the stair above Addy and putting a hand on her shoulder.

"He should be opening them any minute now." Wilmot turned to Addy. "Keep your head down Adeline. We can blend into the darkness, but remember you cannot."

She nodded, ducking her head slightly and peering over the stair rail. Alvis stood to the back of the group, clinging to the wall. Their eyes were locked on the door. "He's coming."

The door opened, and the man walked in. He dripped water onto the rug, shoes squelching with each step. He shut the door behind him, shivering. Every bone in his body was shaking. "Hello? I apologise for the intrusion, but I am a humble merchant wishing to seek shelter from the storm."

"He dresses fine. He might not be as humble as we think." Alvis muttered, but Addy held up a hand, which silenced them.

The man continued. "Please, I will only stay for the night, until the storm passes. I will be gone by morning."

At those words, Addy slowly dropped her hand and knocked on the stairs floor three times. A familiar voice chimed in her head, one that had been a companion to her and the spirits for years.

Another bout of kindness, your majesty?

"Mind your tone. You heard this man. If we shelter him from the storm, he will leave in the morning."

Such kindness from a beast like you.

"Beast in body not in mind. That is what Caris has always told me."

Addy felt Caris' hand squeeze her shoulder at that remark. She closed her eyes again and continued speaking to the castle.

"The sitting room through the right door. Set the fire, place a meal, and he will sleep there for the night. He will be gone by morning. That is his price. And he will pay it."

Shelter for the night and to be gone by morning. A fair price, for saving his life. I accept.

Addy opened her eyes, and the door to the right of the man opened. She could see the amber tones from the fire coming out from the shadows. The man looked into the room, eyes wide. It looked like they were filling with tears.

"Oh bless you, wherever you might be. I thank you for your kindness. May the spirits smile fondly for you." He walked into the room, and the door shut behind him.

"They already do…" Caris whispered to Addy, lifting her hand from her shoulder and standing up. "I will keep watch on our guest for the night."

"There is no need, Caris," Wilmot explained. "This is my duty-,"

She put a hand up to him. "You have stood guard almost every night over this castle. I will watch over him and tend to any needs he has. He might need medicine with how cold he looked. Allow me to do this, please."

"But-,"

"Listen to Caris." Addy stood up herself, with Alvis immediately coming to her aid. "It is late, and there is no point in everyone arguing."

Wilmot bowed his head. "I understand. May we walk you to your quarters Adeline?"

"That would be most kind of you."

Addy looked to Caris, who opened her arms and welcome Addy into a tight embrace. Caris' light hands held her close, and when they lifted their heads again, she kissed Addy on the cheek. "Sleep well, my dear."

"Goodnight Caris."

Alvis and Wilmot offered their arms, and Addy took them. The two helped her up the stairs, and towards her private quarters, which was tucked away in the west wing of the castle. Quarters was a bit of a stretch, as it was only one room. However, Wilmot insisted she takes some pride in her accommodation. The first great step to having confidence in others was to have confidence in yourself.
Wilmot opened the door for her, and Addy stepped inside. Her bedroom was at the teetering edge between messy and clean, a suitable middle ground, considering she was never one to demand perfection. The king-sized bed was covered in throw pillows and blankets of various colours, and the wardrobe door was ajar, showing the limited quantities of clothes that Addy felt comfortable wearing.

"Are you sure you'll be alright tonight Adeline?" Wilmot asked, letting go of her arm as Alvis did the same.

"I'll be fine, and Caris will too. Both of you go and rest, I'll see you in the morning."

"Goodnight, Addy," Alvis said, before vanishing into the air.

Wilmot bowed low and spoke in a soft voice before disappearing. "Farewell."

Addy closed the bedroom door, letting out a long and relaxed breath. There was still that pit of worry in her stomach. She hated having to be the one to make the decision alone. Everyone watching her for guidance, and the nagging feeling that if she made the wrong choice there would be a grave consequence. She tried so hard to be strong, to match her appearance. But compared to what she had become due to the curse, she was nothing.

"Can you turn the light on, please?" She asked aloud, and the three-pointed candelabra sat on the vanity lit up with soft flames.

Addy took off her cloak, flinging it over the vanity chair and sat on the bed. She fell back, sinking into the mound of material and pillow feathers. Her hands trailed up her horns, following the curves around to the sharp point at the end. It was awkward to sleep with them, but Addy had found a way around them. Always adapting, always managing. Never truly living.

However, Addy supposed a cursed life was better than no life at all.

She pushed herself up the bed, nestling her head between the pillows, her horns slotting into the gaps. As if sensing she was drifting off to sleep, she heard the candle flames wink out one by one.

Addy slept and dreamt of nothing.

*****

The beast awoke to the sunrise pouring through the windows. Addy lifted her head, wincing at the light. Her hand went to touch her face, but she stopped herself, remembering the scars on her face and around her eyes. Marks from the times she accidentally cut herself with her now sharp claws. She pushed herself off the bed, regaining her balance as she teetered from the weight of her horns.

The mornings were always slow and tedious, a chance for Addy to repeat the laborious routine she had fallen into.
She thought for a moment that this day would be like any other, but remembered that the castle had an unwanted guest. Addy finished her routine with haste, managing to comb her hair and get dressed. There were heavy circles under her yellow eyes. She threw her green cloak over her shoulders and made her way down the hallway, back towards the main staircase. Caris was already there when Addy arrive, standing on the landing between the two staircases and watching the door where the castle's guest was staying.

Caris noticed Addy immediately, giving her a bright morning smile. She drifted over as Addy sat on the steps.
"Would you like some breakfast, dear?" She asked, putting a hand on Addy's shoulder.

"I'll eat after our guest has left. How was he last night?"

Caris shrugged, her ghostly body shifting as she moved. "Slept through the storm like a baby. Nothing of concern. Alvis took a peek at his cart though."

Addy chuckled, not surprised at Alvis's lack of trust towards the unexpected arrival. "Did they find anything to satisfy their curiosity?"

"They were right to think he was not so humble. He seemed to have lots of fine presents in his cart. Gifts from across the sea."

"He must have been coming back from the port towns, checking on his ships. Perhaps the presents are for his family."

Addy and Caris played this game all the time as Addy grew up. Every time there was a glimpse of someone at the window, Caris would encourage her to create an elaborate story for them.

Caris smiled. "He must be. Alvis explained there was a mix of beautiful dresses and hunting gear. This merchant must have many children. How many do you think he has?"

"Five," Addy said immediately, not thinking about it. "Lots of presents for lots of children. And they must be older if they hunt."

"A humble merchant with five adult children. Anything else you can think of?"

Addy rested her head on her closed hand, biting her lip and continuing to think. "He braved that storm. He must want to get home, back to his children. Makes me think they're a close family, that he truly cares for them."

Unlike Addy's parents, who abandoned her in this castle. If not for the kindness of the dark spirit that cursed her, Addy would be dead.

The door to the right opened, and the merchant stepped out, closing it behind him. Caris waved at Addy to crouch down. He looked brighter than he did last night, his clothes had dried out. There was a healthy glow to his face. He went to the front door, looking back over the staircase one final time.

"I thank you again, for your hospitality and kindness. I hope the spirits find you and gift you many blessings."

Addy held in a scoff. The merchant opened the castle door and disappeared outside. She looked up to Caris, who was watching the door with wide eyes. "Can you help me get to the window? We need to make sure he leaves."

"Of course, dear." She replied, offering Addy her hands. She pulled her to her feet and the two made their way up the steps and around to the front window.

The two of them watched the merchant pull his horse out from the stable, and check his cart was secure. He began to lead his horse by the reins, up the paths towards the castle gates.

But then he stopped. And turned his head to the right.

Towards the rose garden. He let go of the reins and started to walk over there.

"What is he doing?" Caris asked, putting a hand to the window.

"The roses, he must have seen them. I have to stop him, he needs to leave."

"Addy no-,"

"He can't see you, Caris!" She turned away from the window, heading to the stairs. Caris began to quickly chase after her. "He's going to have a debt if he takes a rose."

And nobody should have to pay a debt. Nobody should have the same fate as Addy. She stumbled down the stairs, gripping the rail, her claws digging into the wood and leaving scratch marks on the surface. She knew this castle from the inside out, and as such knew the quickest way to the garden without the merchant seeing her.

The rose garden had become Addy's pride and joy. It was the one thing she could maintain and keep alive, that thrived in the chaos that was her life. There was a servant's door that led outside. Addy swallowed her nerves and trailed through the bushes and hedgerows that made up the garden around the castle. When she saw the roses ahead, she pressed her back against the high bushes, keeping her distance from the merchant.

But she was too late. She saw him pull a rose from the bush, holding it carefully in his hands. Addy felt a deep rumbling in her chest, the castle churning from the betrayal. She moved around the corner, where she could still see the merchant but knew she couldn't be spotted, and prepared herself for what she would have to do next.
She swallowed, taking a deep breath. In her mind, she heard Wilmot's words of encouragement. The reminders that true bravery came from true belief. To play the beast was to play the part, and do whatever she needed to protect herself and what she loved.

As the beast spoke, her voice sounded like it had risen from the depths of hell. "What are you doing?" She demanded.

The merchant leapt back in fright, almost dropping the rose. "Are you the master of this castle? Please I meant no harm, I just wanted-,"

"You made a deal."

"A deal?" The merchant's face paled. "The castle is enchanted, you're a spirit!"

Addy did not want to waste time arguing over the specifics, so continued to explain. "Shelter for the night and to be gone by morning. That was the deal, that was the price you would pay. That rose is not included in that payment."

"I'm sorry, I'm sorry. Please understand I had no idea this was a spirit's castle. If I'd had known-,"

"Knowing or not doesn't matter. You made a promise to myself and the castle that you would leave by morning. Now there is another debt, another price to pay. Do you understand what that means?"

The merchant's face fell, as he looked back down at the rose. "Have mercy please, the rose was for my daughter."

"I don't get to be merciful. The price you must now pay is not up to me."

Addy bent down, knocking on the ground three times. The voice of the castle crept into her head.

Who knew kindness would come at such a cost?

"Silence your whining. Name the price."

Hm. Such a debt. We saved his life and this is how we get repaid? How disappointing.

"Get on with it."

The merchant spun around, confused. "Who are you speaking to?"

A life for a life, your majesty. Someone must take his place.

Addy sighed heavily. Her heaving sounded like a volcano getting ready to erupt. "The castle demands a life for a life. You must bring someone to take the place of the life we saved."

"Someone? A life?" The merchant scowled angrily. "You can't be serious!"

"It is the price. If you do not return to pay it, a grave consequence will occur. You have heard the tales of those who do not pay their debts."

The merchant looked back at the rose. "Fine, I will return. I will pay my debt. Please give me some time."

"Time is a kindness I can offer. Now leave, before more is demanded of you."

The merchant ran off, and Addy remained frozen against the bushes, waiting for as long as possible to make sure he had left. A few minutes later, Wilmot appeared in front of her.

"He's gone, Adeline."

Addy breathed a sigh of relief, sinking to the floor. She put her hands in her face, her voice returning to normal. "I never want to do that again."

"But you did so well Adeline! You sounded very intimidating. I would have been trembling, if I could still tremble." Wilmot responded, kneeling in front of her.

She chuckled, rolling her eyes. "It made me feel so icky inside."

"Such personalities will make us feel that way. You offered him great kindness even by trying to stop him. But we can't make up for foolish choices."

Addy shook her hands, wincing at every aspect of the interaction that occurred between her and the merchant. Almost as if she was trying to shake off the uncomfortable feelings. "Ugh, never again. Never, never, never again."

Alvis suddenly appeared next to Wilmot, standing over the two of them. "You did an excellent job and played the part very well. He's well off into the forest now."

Addy paused, a thought appearing in her head. "He's not coming back is he?"

Alvis chuckled, shaking their head. "Nope."

Her arms flopped to her sides. "Spirits damned it."

Chapter 3

Actions, Meet Consequences

Bellerose

The sun rose again, as it always does over Reverie. The same sun, in the same position every morning. Sometimes, it would reveal different colours, but that happened less than one might think. At this time, Belle would be getting ready to go to work, eager to leave her siblings behind. However, today was the first time, in a long time, where that did not happen. Instead, she woke up, crept past her slumbering sisters, and decided to clean up before her father returned home from his trip.

There was a strange melancholy in the silence of the house, something Belle had never been around the witness. She could feel it weighing on her as the hours ticked by, as she tried to make up more things to do. It was not like she had anywhere to go now. Even if she did attempt to leave the house, she would immediately withdraw from all the shameful looks the townspeople would give her.

Such was the price of rejecting love.

As luck, or fate would have it, Belle heard the sounds of a horse and cart approaching the house. She rushed to the door, swinging it wide open. Her face lit up when she saw her father sitting in the front seat of the cart. She rushed out to him as he climbed down, and the two tightly embraced.

"I'm so happy you made it home!" Belle joyfully exclaimed. "Here, let me help you empty the cart-,"

"No! No, there's no need Belle." Her father put his hands up to her. "I will sort the cart in a moment. After all, I have...gifts for my children. Let us go inside, perhaps you could pour me some tea."

Belle wondered for a moment why her father was hesitating. He was usually so firm in his words, knowing exactly what he wanted to say. But, she shrugged it off as exhaustion and helped him inside. Once they were in the kitchen and Belle was preparing the tea, she started asking her father about the journey.

"So, I want to know everything. How were the ships? Where had they been? Did you hear any interesting stories?"

Her father chuckled. "So many questions in one breath. Has there not been enough excitement here while I've been gone? Did you not go out with your sisters?"

Belle poured him a cup of tea, and one for herself. "Mira and Clara did not want to be seen with me. I've been bored out of my skull. In a not-so-shocking revelation, I enjoyed the stimulation my job at the library gave me."

"Well, you could have kept that job, and you know that."

She sighed, sipping her tea. "I stand by my decision."

Her father's smile had a bitterness behind it. "I know you do. I hope you don't live to regret it."

One of the bedroom doors opened. Eder and Faron announced they had heard two voices, and welcomed their father home. More tea was poured, all by Belle, as her brothers were caught up to speed with what had happened on their father's trip. Belle's father answered every question with enthusiasm, a courtesy he had never granted to her. Her sisters emerged from the other bedroom not a moment later, delightfully taking a turn to kiss their father on the forehead and thank the spirits he was home safely. Now that her father was distracted, Belle took notice of mannerisms she had not noticed before. There was an eagerness to her father as if he was trying to mask something by projecting joy. There was something he was not telling them.

Her father rose from the dining room table. "Now, since you're all here, I best get out the gifts I brought home to you!"

Mira clapped her hands together, an excited smile on her face. "Oh, I have been waiting for this!"

Clara put a hand on Mira's arm. "I wonder if it is something we can wear for our weddings!"

Belle chuckled as she muttered to herself. "If he brought you home white dresses they will be stained with mud."

Her father went outside for a moment, and bit by bit, he brought in a suitcase of gorgeous dresses for Mira and Clara. The two girls squealed in ridiculously loud delight, holding up the fine garments to each other. They began to quietly squabble over who would get which item of clothing, and which they could agree to share. For her brothers, a case of the finest hunting gear. Freshly carved bows and finely pointed arrows.

Sharp daggers in leather sleeves. The twin boys were overjoyed, already discussing what of their old gear they could pawn off to make some extra coin.

Belle was last, as always. As her father walked up to her, she noticed his hesitation. The pause as he lifted the rose to her, placing it in her delicate fingers. "And for you my dear. My safe return...and a rose."

She looked down at the rose, her eyes leaving her father's puzzling expression. It was like nothing she had ever seen before. Usually, when her father brought home a rose, it had already begun to dry out and wilt from the journey. Right now, it was not the season for them, and Belle always expected the roses she was given to have already lost a little bit of life. But this rose? It was pristine, *perfect*. As if magically preserved to stand the tests of weather and time. The perfect blood red colour. The perfect amount of curves on the petals. A perfect stem with barely any thorns. Almost too perfect.

"Father, where did you get this?" She asked, still looking down at the perfect, perfect rose.

Immediately, her father's tone was defensive. "Never mind where I got it. It's my gift to you, as promised."

"Seriously Belle, it's a rose. Calm down." Mira added, rolling her eyes as she admired a pair of silk gloves. "What's wrong with it?"

"A rose at this time of year should not look like this..." Belle replied, lifting her eyes to her father. His face looked wracked with guilt. "How did you get this rose?"

"There's no need to ask such questions, Belle. I'm home, and I will remain home. That's all that matters."

Belle put the rose in the glass vase on the dining table. "You have not been yourself since you came back. Did something happen while you were gone?"

Eder groaned. "Belle, seriously? He's fine."

"Exactly Eder. I'm fine Belle. You're worrying too much. This is what happens when you don't have something to occupy yourself." He put her hands on her arms, chuckling and shaking his head. "Now, why don't you and I go to the market to find something for dinner, hm?"

Clara made a shooing notion with her free hand towards the door. "Go out with Father, that will sort you out."

Belle stepped back, forcing her father to drop his hands. "If you don't tell me what happened I'll go and find out for myself."

Silence fell across the room. Her father sighed, sitting back down at the table. He put his face in his hands. "I have a debt with a spirit over that rose."

Mira put a hand to her forehead. "A debt?! A spirit's debt?"

"Yes. I did not want to worry my children, but I suppose you must know."

Everyone sat down at the table. Faron a hand on his father's shoulder. "Tell us what happened."

And tell them everything he did. He explained about the storm, the castle, and the mysterious master who offered him a room for the night. The morning after, when a voice told him he now had an unpaid debt over a single rose.

"If I'd had known it was a spirit's castle, I would have never agreed to stay the night."

Clara dabbed her eyes with a handkerchief. "How could you have known? None of us have ever heard of such a castle."

Eder triumphantly stood up from the table. "Well I say Faron and I go there and give the spirit a piece of our mind! How dare they trick you, Father?"

"Sit down Eder. There is no need for that." Her father replied, waving a hand.

Eder dropped back into his seat, looking grumpy. "Then what are we going to do?"

"Nothing." Her father declared, lifting his head to look at all his children. "This spirit never showed their face to me, so they must either be weak, a coward, or both. The price of the debt is nothing of consequence, and I never told the spirit who I was or where I came from. We can continue as normal."

Belle had been silently listening to her father's story. She folded her hands together, as she stared at the perfect rose. "What was the price?"

"As I told you, Belle, nothing of consequence. A debt we can avoid paying."

"We shouldn't ignore this. The spirits know everything and remember everything too." Belle stood up from the table. "What about the Arnold family? One debt to a spirit was left unpaid, and now they can't grow crops on their fields."

Her father sighed. "I'm sure the debt was a difficult one to pay. And besides, we do not have to worry about such things. I believe the spirit was trying to trick me. A debt over a rose is ridiculous."

"That rose could have meant something to the spirit. You have no idea what that castle was, who it belonged to,"

Clara stood up, turning sharply to Belle. "We should be grateful our father is home alive. That is all. Please, no more talk of spirits, or debts."

"Precisely Clara, thank you." Belle's father rose from his seat. "I will go to the market by myself to find us something for dinner. I do not want any of you to worry. You do not need to concern yourself with such worldly matters."

"But-," Belle began to protest but was silenced by her father's glare.

"Please my dear, leave it be. I will be back soon."

Her father walked out the door, heading towards the marketplace. Mira and Clara got up from the table. "Come sister, we can sort through our wardrobe. After all, we have a wedding to plan!"

The sisters laughed and headed back into the bedroom. The twins stood up from the table as well. "We're going

to go and see what we can trade in of our old gear,"
Faron explained.

Eder shoved his old hunting boots onto his feet. "We'll
find Father on the way and help him carry everything."

Faron saw Belle's expression. The worry that had
seemed to find its way forever stuck to her face.
"Seriously, Belle. It is not something to be worrying
over. Most of the time, spirits never collect their debts."

"I can see you're scared too, Faron. Even if you hide it."

He sighed. "Do you want to come with us?"

"No, thank you."

"Alright. Come on Eder, let's head out."

Her brothers left, and Belle, once again, found herself
in dull silence. Behind the closed bedroom door, she
could hear her sisters giggling. An idle joy Belle never
fully understood. She leaned forward and took the
perfect rose out of the vase. Even now, as it sat inside
away from the sun, it had not lost its shine. She hoped
that her father was exaggerating, that such a debt had
not been made over a single rose. If it had, it was
Belle's fault. And she knew that guilt would swallow
her whole.

*****

Spirits be damned.

Spirits be strong.

Spirits come when the nights are long.

At the break of morning, Belle was woken by a loud crashing sound. She had barely slept anyway. The thoughts of the spirits and the debt were swirling around her mind. Her sisters had also been woken up by the commotion. Belle quickly got dressed, and the three of them clumsily made their way out of the bedroom to see what was going on.

Belle's father stood in the doorway, cursing under his breath as he ran outside. Her brothers were already outside, and the sisters watched in horror as they realised what had happened.

The cart, and all of the goods inside, were destroyed. Scattered across the front of the house were broken bits of wood and timber. The wheels of the cart were snapped clean in half. The horse was being comforted by Faron. Belle pushed past Mira and Clara, who stood frozen in fear. The cold air pierced her skin, as she rushed to her father, who was assessing the damage.

"What happened?" Eder asked. "We all heard the loud crash and then…"

"I don't know." Her father was shaking his head. "It was a clear night, there was no storm."

"Maybe an animal?"

"No, an animal would not do this much…"

"Father. The debt." Belle pointed to the carriage. This was no damage from a storm, or an animal, or anything human. There was nothing to be salvaged from what her father brought home yesterday. "This is because of the debt."

"Belle, not now⁻,"

"No!" She stamped her foot on the ground. "What was the price of the debt?"

"You don't understand."

"Make me understand!" She demanded again. Her siblings' faces were pale as she screamed at her father. "What is the price?"

There was no joy in her father's face as he looked around the destruction. Of the consequences of his actions. "A life for a life. In exchange for saving my life, someone would take my place at the castle."

Belle shook her head. "You…"

"Father!" Mira cried out, covering her mouth as tears formed in her eyes. "Who would do such a thing?"

Clara pulled her sister in for a hug, comforting her. Eder and Faron didn't move.

Belle put her face in her hands. "You…"

"Listen, Belle. Everything will be fine."

"You IDIOT!"

Her siblings gasped, and her father's face fell as those words left her mouth. But Belle didn't care, she stormed back inside, pushing past her sisters who still lingered in the doorway. She grabbed her pale blue cloak from the hook and put it on. She also pulled on her boots and grabbed the perfect rose from the table. Her father chased in after her, forcing her sisters to retreat into the corner.

"Belle, what are you doing?" Her father asked, tears forming in his eyes.

"I'm going to pay the debt."

"What?!"

Eder came to her side as she stormed back out of the house. "Belle, be rational."

"I am being rational!" She yelled in his face. "The only reason there is a debt is because of the rose. I'm going to deal with this."

She pulled her cloak tighter around her shoulders. Her father caught up with her, grabbing her hand and trying to pull her back. "Please, I can't lose you to this. You have such a bright future, such a great life. I cannot allow you to give that all away over a rose."

Belle turned her head away, rolling her eyes furiously. "A bright future? A great life? Father, you have made it very clear that I have lost my job, rejected a chance at marriage. And above all, this debt is over a rose I asked for!"

"I-," Her father hesitated. "This is not that simple."

Belle pulled her hand away. "Will you pay the debt then?"

"Well..."

"Just as I thought." Belle sighed, and put a hand on her father's shoulder "I will go deal with this so that you can live happily."

Her father held her for a long time when he pulled away, he smiled softly at her. "You shouldn't have to do this."

"Yes, but none of you will."

Her father said nothing. Her siblings said nothing. All this did was solidify Belle's choice.

She turned, and in the middle of the night, Belle walked to the castle.

Chapter 4

A Meeting of Sorts

Adeline

Addy sat in her usual seat by the window, a book open in her lap. Everything was making her annoyed today. This feeling often came and went, much like the waves of an ocean. She had never seen an ocean, but she had seen enough pictures in books to get a general understanding.

When this feeling arrived, it felt like pain to an unfathomable amount. Addy and her guardians had never worked out whether this was a part of the curse or Addy's mind.

But everything hurt. Physically, emotionally.

Even now, when she looked up at Wilmot, she had to hide a grimace. He apologised for disturbing her but said he had news.

"The first of the consequences has begun. For the merchant, you saved a couple of nights ago."

Addy was quiet for a moment. "How bad was it?"

"Not as bad as it could be, but you know it will get worse."

She closed the book in her lap and moved her legs to sit upright. She winced at the movement, and Wilmot flinched, ready to assist her. Addy put a hand up to stop him. "The castle did ask a steep price."

"And you would think by now people would pay it."

"He had children to get home to, Wil. He was being a good father. I especially can't fault him for that."

Wilmot was silent, and Addy looked up at him, frowning. "You have something to say. You know you can speak freely."

He crossed his arms. "I do not blame you for showing kindness, Adeline. But I ask that you be careful in the future. Some would mistake your kindness for foolishness."

"I understand. I'll be careful."

The door to the library burst open, slamming against the wall. Alvis stood there, their eyes wide with fear. They gasped heavily. "Somebody is approaching the castle!"

"Again?" Wilmot exclaimed.

"I saw them from the upstairs window."

"Wil, help me to my feet," Addy asked, holding her taloned hands out towards Wilmot. As he gracefully pulled her up from the window seat, she looked at Alvis. "How far away are they?"

"I'm not sure-,"

Caris appeared from behind Alvis, almost pushing past them to look into the library. There was sadness in her eyes. "Addy...there's a woman here. She says she's come to pay the debt."

*****

"Spirit! I summon thee! I've come to pay my father's debt!"

Addy stood behind one of the stone pillars on the upper landing. Down below, at the bottom of the grand staircase, stood a young woman. She paced back and forth, shouting at the top of her lungs.

"She thinks it's a spirit who asked for the debt...must be what the merchant told her," Alvis whispered, standing opposite Addy.

"Well, this castle is a spirit." Caris added, leaning over the stone bannister to watch the unexpected visitor.

"This castle is working for power even we cannot comprehend. A spirit who started all of this." Wilmot explained, rubbing his chin.

Caris turned back. "It was Addy's parents that started this."

"Now's not the time." Addy snapped, unaware of her tone at that moment. She knocked on the column three times.

Ah. What an unexpected twist, hm? How do you feel about the new arrival, your majesty?

"Quiet. If she is here, is the debt paid?"

I am satisfied. I will tell her when she can leave.

Addy took a long, deep breath, a despairing pit forming in her stomach and chest. "I need to speak with her."

"Are you sure Addy?" Caris put a hand on her arm. "She might…"

"I know, but she's going to be living with a beast. Might as well get the fear and hatred out of the way."

Addy pushed herself off the column and slowly started to make her way down the stairs. She slowed her breathing, feeling the switch into that low, sinister voice. The same she had used on the merchant only two nights ago.

"Would you kindly stop shouting?" She announced, stopping on the first landing, before the next set of stairs.

The young woman turned to look at Addy.

And Addy looked at her, and only for a second, she thought of roses.

The new arrival to the castle was wearing a pastel blue dress with a white ruffled top. The skirt was covered in a pattern of light pink and lilac flowers. The mud and dirt from the forest had splattered the skirt hem and her brown boots. Her chestnut hair was ruffled by the wind, even though it had been tied back by a blue ribbon. Curls of hair were framing her round face and pink cheeks. Her dark brown eyes pierced Addy's, but the moment she saw the beast in front of her, fear entered her pupils.

"I-I've come to pay my father's debts."

"I know. Could your father not pay it himself?"

The young woman avoided Addy's firm gaze. "No. He needed to be home. For my brothers and sisters."

"I see," Addy replied, trying to ignore what was stirring inside of her at that moment. She carried on walking down the next set of stairs.

The woman thrust out her hand, revealing a rose. The one from Addy's garden. "He got the rose for me. I asked him for it. This is my debt to pay, and if I have to stay here for the rest of my life to pay it, I will. But I ask you spirit, to leave my family alone."

Addy paused at the bottom of the stairs, her hand on the stone bannister. "I am no spirit. The castle is the spirit who asked for the debt. I am simply its resident."

"You didn't do this?"

"You could call me a negotiator," Awkwardly, Addy stopped before this young woman, plucking the rose from her grasp. She lowered her voice, and it almost went back to normal. Her voice wavered like it never had before. "You can still leave. There's time."

The young woman shook her head frantically. "No. I have to do this, for my family. I will pay this debt."

Addy felt a shiver of nerves crackle down her spine. She took a breath, steadying her voice. Trying to remain in control. "What reason does your father have for not paying it himself? He knew what he was doing when he asked for shelter."

The woman's stern expression shifted and she didn't meet Addy's eyes for a second. "It's my fault. He did nothing wrong. He was trying to get home. Surely a being such as yourself can find no fault in that?"

A being. Not a human. Addy tried to ignore how hearing those words made her feel.

She lifted a clawed hand towards the woman, offering a handshake. "My name is Addy."

The new resident of the castle took a step back, recoiling in surprise. "You're a woman."

Addy tried to hide her disappointment in how she reacted. She kept her hand outstretched. "Did you think only men could be this beastly?"

"N-no, I-," The woman did not take Addy's hand. "I'm Belle."

"Belle."

Addy repeated, the name settling on her lips. She turned away, not wanting to look at Belle.

It was starting to become painful. As she turned, Addy stumbled, her legs twisting. She fell forward, the weight of her body pulling her down. She managed to grab the bannister in time.

"Addy!"

Caris, Alvis and Wilmot appeared suddenly at the bottom of the stairs. Caris had a hand on Addy's back, helping her stand upright. Belle, in her defence, screamed at the sudden appearance of the spirits and took several steps back.

Wilmot put his hands up. "Ma'am do not be alarmed-,"

"This castle does have spirits!" Belle protested, pointing threateningly at all of them.

Alvis rolled their eyes. "There are spirits everywhere."

"Not now, Alvis." Addy lifted her head, trying to maintain her composure. She looked over her shoulder back at Belle.

"You are not a prisoner here, this is now your home as much as mine. Knock anywhere in the castle three times, and the castle will give you what you ask for. By staying here, you will clear the debt. The castle will tell you when it is paid."

Belle didn't respond. Addy nodded to Caris. "Could you and Alvis please show our new guest around, and where her room is?"

"Of course, Addy. Wilmot, take her back to her room to rest."

Addy and Belle's eyes met. "If it is any comfort, I am sorry we met like this. I hope your father knows how much of a sacrifice you made."

"My father isn't a bad person." She replied defiantly. "If circumstances were different, he would have paid this debt. He would have done it, I know it."

Addy started to walk up the stairs, with Wilmot beside her. "You keep telling yourself that."

Chapter 5
A Warmer Welcome
Bellerose

Belle watched Addy leave.

Addy. Such a human name for a monstrous figure. She couldn't get over the appearance of the beast, who seemed to be the owner of this castle. Those twisting, arching horns. Sharp green eyes that felt like they could stab her. A disfigured face with high cheekbones and skin that looked like tree bark. No wonder Addy couldn't keep her balance for long. And no wonder she only had spirits to comfort her

Speaking of spirits, one of the figures that had appeared at the bottom of the stairs. Alvis, if she remembered correctly, held out a hand to her.

"May I take your cloak then, Miss Belle?"

Belle hesitated, realising the spirit had no face, only white hollow eyes. She hugged herself, gripping her arms tight.

Alvis dropped their hand. "Never mind then."

The other spirit nudged Alvis. "Our Addy was the same when we first appeared." She turned to Belle. "Don't mind them dear, you'll get used to them. I'm Caris, this is Alvis. The knightly figure you saw is Wilmot. Other visitors come now and then, who I'm sure you'll meet in time. Now, would you like a tour?"

Caris had such a motherly presence that it was startling. Belle remained frozen, struggling to take it all in. The spirit sighed, putting a hand on her transparent cheek.

"Listen, dear. You're safe here. Nothing is going to harm you or wish you harm. You are a brave lass for paying your father's debt, and while you are here, you will be cared for."

Belle took a step back, continuing to cradle herself. "I've heard the stories about what you spirits do. How do I know this is not some trick?"

"Goodness Miss Belle, if want to go ahead and believe every story you read, I'll lock you in the library," Caris added, now putting her hands on her hips.

She didn't have hips, but the expression still stood. Caris continued, outstretching a hand that looked like needles. "Now, I am more than happy to leave you to it, or I can show you where everything is so you can get settled in as a guest."

Belle let out a long sigh. She looked around the entranceway to the castle and the door. She knew that if she turned around and left, the consequences for her family would continue. She had to follow through with this, even as the fear crippled her where she stood.

She reached up and took off her cloak. Alvis reached out a hand once more, and she passed it over to them. Alvis grinned. "I'll call this our unofficial icebreaker. Caris, I leave Miss Belle with you. I will go prepare her room."

They disappeared in a wisp of mist and smoke. Caris tilted her head towards the staircase, gesturing for

Belle to follow her. "Now then, let us begin the tour."

*****

As it turns out, the castle had a lot of rooms. Most of them weren't in use, with Caris explaining that Addy had grown out of the splendour she was raised in. Everyone had agreed to cover up any rooms that weren't being used. The exception now was that Alvis was finishing preparing the room that would become Belle's bedroom.

Belle followed behind Caris, listening and asking as many questions as she could think of. Her brothers would often tell her that curiosity was her greatest annoying trait, but Caris didn't seem to mind.

"Why is this castle falling apart if you all live here?" Belle asked as Caris pointed out another dust-covered room that wasn't being used.

Caris waved a hand in dismissal. "The castle, or should I say the spirit of the castle, is a notorious grump. Addy has tried many times to get it to repair itself, but it refuses, saying it's the wrong time."

"Addy can talk to the castle?"

"Yes, remember what she said? Knock three times if you need anything. But Miss Belle, I ask that you are careful. The castle is a grump, but it's also mischievous. Be clear about what you want." Caris stopped at a set of double doors. "Ah! Now this is an exciting room."

Caris pushed open the doors, revealing a library. Belle let her jaw drop. There were rows upon rows of bookshelves. A fireplace sat in the middle of the room, with two window seats on either side. There was even a stepladder to reach the higher shelves. On an oak table, were piles of opened books and papers, with a map stretched out across the surface. The room was lit by sunlight, and golden candelabras sat on the walls for when the night came. The shelves were covered in painted gold leaves and engravings of curving, swooshing lines. It was clear this room was well-loved.

"What do you think?" Caris asked, smiling amusingly at Belle's expression.

"I have no words."

Caris stepped inside, gesturing to the shelves. "Now, Alvis knows these shelves better than I do, they can help you find something if you ever need it."

Belle walked towards the shelves but stopped herself. Out of the corner of her eye, she noticed one of the window seats. The pillows were all over the place, and there was a blanket draping down to the floor. She pointed to it. "Does someone sit there usually?"

Caris turned to see what Belle was pointing at. "Ah, yes. That's Addy's favourite spot to read."

"She...Addy reads?"

If Caris could blink in confusion, she would. "Y-yes Addy reads. She's read almost every book here."

"Is...what kind of..." Belle paused, struggling to find the words. "What is she like?"

Caris let out a heavy sigh. "Are you wondering if you should be scared, Miss Belle?"

"It's that obvious?" Belle replied. She felt her cheeks burn with embarrassment.

"You had a look in your eyes when you first saw Addy. I've seen it before."

"She looks…"

"I know how she looks," Caris replied, almost snapping back at Belle. "None of this is her fault, dear. None of it. Addy is a kind soul. Her appearance does not match her heart."

"It seemed it did when she spoke to me."

Caris stepped forward. Her eyes glowed as she stared at Belle. "Sometimes, we all have to perform. I'm sure you've had to do it as well."

Belle didn't respond.

Caris went back to the door. "I'll take you to your room now. Let you get settled in. One quick thing, your room is in the east wing. The west wing is where Addy's bedroom is. I politely ask that you respect her privacy and not go there."

Caris had turned her head to see if Belle understood. She nodded. As they walked towards the east wing, a silence had settled. Caris was somebody who saw whoever was beneath the beast. Even though Belle could not see it, she tried to see Caris' perspective. Tried, and failed.

They reached another set of doors, at the end of the hallway, which Caris opened to reveal a bedroom. It was almost twice the size of the room Belle shared with her sisters. There was a large bed on one side, covered in baby blue bedsheets and pillows. A white wardrobe and dressing table were on the other, with a golden mirror on a stand. The cream curtains were drawn open, as the sun began to bring in the evening. Caris walked inside, and picked up the candelabra on the dressing table, waving a hand over the wicks. The flames flickered to life instantly. On the bed, was Belle's cloak, along with a small pile of books.

"Ah, Alvis must have picked you a few titles," Caris explained, as she checked the inside of the wardrobe. "And found you some clothes!"

Belle looked over Caris' shoulder and saw that, true enough, the wardrobe was filled with an assortment of clothes and outfits.

"I'll leave you to get settled in." She continued and pointed to the clock on the wall. "Dinner is in an hour, but I think I'll bring it to your room tonight."

"I would appreciate that. Thank you."

Caris nodded, drifting towards the door. She looked back at Belle. "If you need anything, I'm around. You can usually call one of us and we'll hear you. Or knock three times."

Belle nodded. "Thank you, Caris."

"I hope you do enjoy your time here dear, however long that may be. It's been a long time since Addy has had such company."

She went to leave, but Caris turned back around. "Can you promise me something?"

She shrugged her shoulders, unsure of what to say.

"Be kind to Addy. See beyond the beast."

She froze. Caris spoke about Addy with such fondness. A fondness Belle couldn't comprehend. This was the person who stood by idle while passing on the message that her father now owned an unimaginable debt. A debt with great consequences, power from worlds not under anyone's control. Her voice, the way she spoke to her father and Belle. Even as she stumbled up those stairs, it was a beast on those stairs. Belle, despite her better judgement, could not see past it.

Caris shook her head, giving Belle a vague smile. "Maybe not a promise, but can you try?"

Belle nodded. "I'll try."

"Okay. I'll be back soon with your dinner."

"Thank you."

Caris closed the door, and Belle immediately walked to the windows, trying to see what she could outside her window. It was a long way down, and the forest stretched infinitely around her. Even though she knew there was no going home, there was comfort in at least trying to work out an escape plan.

Belle sat on the bed, but sank to the floor, curling her knees against her chess. One of her hands grazed the hardwood floor. Then she remembered what Addy and Caris had told her. She curled her hand into a fist and knocked on the floor three times.

Ah, I was wondering when you would introduce yourself.

Belle let out a cry, as a voice as eerie and sinister as death latched into her skull, echoing in her brain. It spoke without sentience, without form. A voice in her head.

"W-what?"

I admit, this is somewhat entertaining. I forget there is always the shock of the first encounter.

"You're the castle?"

Yes. What a pretty price to pay for a rose, hm? What did you say your name was?"

"Belle."

Belle. What do you need Belle?

Belle thought for a moment. "When can I go home?"

Not yet.

"When can I see my family?"

Not yet.

She huffed. "You're being vague on purpose."

Rightly observed. Now, do you need something or was this just to see if you were being lied to?

She paused. "There's a blanket I had on my bed at home. A pink one. Can I have it?"

Are you sure you want something so simple?

"Is there a price?"

No. She made it very clear that you were living here and I should not ask for a price for anything you ask.

"Then I would like that. Please."

As you wish.

Belle's head was silent once more. She stood up, and as she did, she noticed something new had appeared on the bed.

A worn, fraying, familiar pink blanket.

She picked it up in her arms, holding it close to her face. It smelled like her sisters' perfumes and powder. Belle crawled onto the bed, curling into a ball as the tears fell down her face.

She stayed that way for a long time.

*****

A few days passed.

Belle hadn't dared to venture outside her room. Caris took the hint, continuing to bring her meals to the bedroom instead of asking her to go to the dining room. She spent the time reading the books Alvis had left her, and watching the sprawling forest from the windows.

One evening, as she watched the sunset, there was a knock at her bedroom door.

"Come in." She announced, turning her head to the door.

To her surprise, it wasn't Caris with her dinner like usual. Instead, the spirit Wilmot stood in her doorway, hands behind his back.

He bowed in greeting. "Miss Belle, I trust you are well. I've come to escort you to dinner."

Belle raised an eyebrow, stepping away from the window and towards Wilmot. "What are you talking about?"

He lifted his head and pushed his shoulders back to stand up straighter. "We thought it would be nice for you to get out of this room for a while. Also, Adeline is feeling better after a few rough days. Everyone agreed the two of you having dinner together might...help break the tension."

"Adeline?" Belle asked but then realised who Wilmot meant. "Oh, Addy."

"Yes. Apologies I default to using her full name, a force of habit. Nonetheless, it would be my pleasure to escort you to the dining room."

Belle thought for a moment about protesting, about insisting she stay here. But, though she was reluctant to admit it, she was getting a bit sick of this room. If she had to stay here for an undefined amount of time, perhaps she could play along with the spirits' attempts at hospitality.

Besides, Belle had told Caris she would try.

Wilmot offered Belle his arm, which she took, looping her own through his elbow. He smiled. "Wonderful, I am most grateful."

*****

Wilmot pushed open the door to the dining room, allowing Belle to step in by herself. It was a grand affair, much like the rest of the castle. Even though the walls had seen better days, the table was still in good shape, despite a few scratches and scuff marks. Above the table was a golden chandelier that was lit, brightening up the windowless room.

At the other end of the table, Addy looked up, noticed Belle, and clumsily stood up.

Belle swallowed the lump in her throat and spoke, her voice sounding alien to her. "H-hello."

Addy seemed to open her mouth to speak, but no words came out at first. She let out a loose breath. "They didn't tell me you were joining me." She explained, her eyes glancing over to Wilmot, who stood at the door.

He said nothing, and nodded to Belle, stepping out and closing the door behind him. Belle's dinner was already at the seat set out for her, so she put a hand on the chair. "I can leave if you would prefer it."

"No!" Addy called out from the other side of the room. She must have realised how loud she was and spoke her next sentence at a softer volume. "No. Please stay."

Belle sat down. Addy soon followed but didn't continue eating, only poking at parts of her plate with her fork. Belle began to eat, periodically looking up at Addy, who appeared more sinister in the candlelight. She was wearing a loose dark blue dress, which surprised Belle. The long sleeves had been rolled up to Addy's elbows. Her brown hair was braided down one shoulder, her horns protruding out of the top of her head, causing the braid to fall apart in various places.

Every time Addy noticed Belle was looking at her, she looked away.

If there was a definition for an awkward situation, this would be it.

After a long silence, Belle spoke again. "Wilmot said you have been unwell the past few days."

Addy froze and looked up. It took her a moment to respond. "Yes, I'm afraid I was somewhat incapacitated."

Belle noticed that Addy was so hesitant when she spoke. Was she nervous?

"Are you feeling better?"

"I'm getting there. I appreciate the concern." Addy quickly replied, looking back at her food. There was another beat of silence. "Is your room alright? We wanted to make sure you were comfortable."

"It is perfectly fine. Not what I expected, but it is fine, thank you."

Addy lifted her head, and Belle felt those horrid yellow eyes lock onto her. "What did you expect?"

Belle suddenly felt uncomfortable, a bitterness settling on her tongue and in her stomach. "Considering where we are and...the kind of...thing you are."

Addy's cutlery clattered against her plate as it fell from her sickly clawed hands. "I see."

"I thought it would be a different situation." Belle continued, trying to ignore the look of horror on Addy's face. "That's all."

"A different situation?" Addy asked, pushing further, much to Belle's discomfort. "You are making little sense, Belle."

Belle refused to take more of this interrogation and stood up from the table. Her chair made a loud groan as it dragged across the wood. "I shouldn't have to explain myself to something like you."

Addy sat up, slowly getting up out of her chair. Her mouth was opening, ready to spew words, but she wasn't speaking. Belle shook her head. "Thank you for dinner."

Belle stormed out of the room and retreated to her bedroom. She couldn't shake the feeling of pure disgust that had now inhabited her entire being. Every time she looked at Addy, all she could think was what horrible atrocities she must have done to become...that beast.

All the spirits Addy must have angered, and the price she paid for it.

"She called me a *thing*!"

Addy sat on the dining room table, legs dangling awkwardly off the edge as Caris cleaned up the plates and cutlery from dinner. Her emotions were indescribable, a negativity she had never experienced before. Deeper than the despair of her curse.

Caris turned around, passing off the dishes to Wilmot, who took them into the kitchen. She walked to Addy, reaching for her hands. Addy gripped Caris' hands tightly, her emotions building. "Am I not even worthy of being called a person to her?"

"Addy-,"

"Do people in this world hate so easily? Even when they have nothing to base it on. Is this what happens, usually?"

Before Caris could respond, Alvis phased through the main dining room door. "Miss Belle is safely back in her room." They must have noticed Addy's frantic expression. "Goodness, what have I missed?"

Caris looked over at Alvis, narrowing her eyes, almost to dissuade them from asking. Addy interrupted the silent interaction. "Belle called me a thing."

"A-a thing? Apologies what thing did she call you? Be specific." Alvis asked, casually meandering towards them.

"No, it-," Addy flicked her wrists, letting out an exasperated sigh. "She called me a something, not a someone."

"Oh. I see."

"And Addy, naturally, is upset." Caris finished.

"I can see that," Alvis replied in a mutter. They raised their voice to a normal speaking volume. "Did you say anything to her to make her insult you?"

Addy looked shocked, and Caris smacked their arm. "Alvis!"

"It is a legitimate question!" They snapped back, crossing their arms.

Caris scowled and began to scold them. "You should know Addy-,"

"Caris." Addy cut her off with a firm tone. "I am not a child any more. If Alvis wishes to be honest, they can be."

Caris relented, pulling out one of the dining room chairs and taking a seat. Wilmot came back into the room at that point, leaving behind a trail of water droplets and soap suds. He leaned against the wall.

Before he could interrupt the conversation once more, Alvis began to carry on their point. "I ask the hard questions with a kind heart Addy, you know I do. You have not interacted with someone your age...ever.

Spirits above and below, the last time you interacted with a human was on your tenth birthday, and we all know how that went."

Addy listened to their words carefully. She crossed her rotten wooden fingers together, the claws now resting on her palms. "I don't believe I said anything that would insult her. I admit maybe I pushed a little on some of her comments but that was only because I was curious."

Alvis sat next to Addy on the dining table surface and took her hand, squeezing it affectionately. "Humans are complicated, Addy. You know that as much as I do. And as much as you wish for you and Belle to get along, it is going to take time."

Her eyes lifted upwards to meet theirs. "But I do not know how much time we have. The last thing I wish is for Belle to leave here spreading tales of the horrific beast in the castle."

The comment made Wilmot chuckle, as he finally decided to have his say. "Humans fear first, question second, and love last." He paused, a smile forming on his lips. "Do you remember Miss Lilith? She was only here for a week, and the first time she saw you, she screamed!"

The memory of that moment came back to Addy suddenly. The fond times she shared with the castle's mysterious and temporary guest.

Caris beamed. "Oh Miss Lilith was a character...but Wil is right, Addy. You need a bit of patience."

Alvis continued to hold her hand. "Why do you want Belle to like you so badly?"

Addy shrugged, a frown forming on her scarred face. "To put it simply, what if she is the last human I get to talk to?"

Caris tutted, shaking her head. "Now Addy, don't be so cynical."

"It's true though Caris!" She whipped her head around to look at her, letting go of Alvis' hand. "What if this curse does kill me before it's reversed? This world will remember me as the beast in the castle, the monster who kept a poor woman here to pay a debt from a rose. I...I do not want to become the villain of my story."

Caris sighed and stood up, walking over to kiss Addy softly on the forehead. "You would never be the villain of any story Adeline."

Addy leaned towards Caris, who pulled her into her ghostly arms and held her close. Caris continued speaking in a gentle tone. "All you can do is be yourself. Show Belle a little kindness, and I'm sure she'll change her tune."

Alvis stood up from the dining table as Addy pulled away from Caris' embrace. They offered an arm to Addy, which she took. "To the library?"

"Yes, please."

"As you wish."

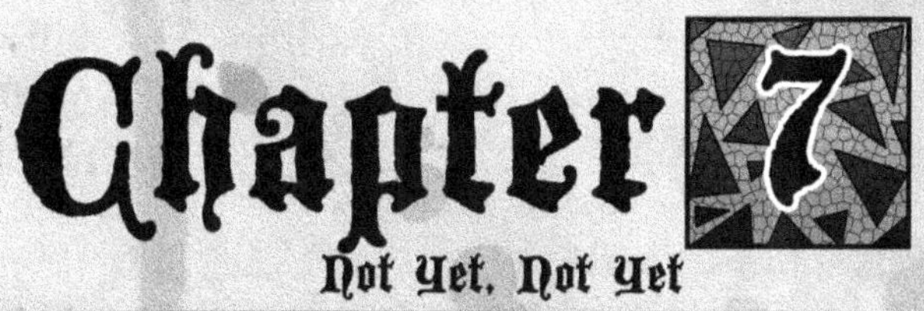

Chapter 7

Not Yet, Not Yet

Bellerose

It had taken Belle an entire week to muster the courage to leave her room again. A whole week of frantic pacing, hatching escape plans and theorising about all manner of curses. Caris had brought every meal to her room, the spirit finally getting the message about Belle not wanting to be in the same room as Addy.

Be kind. What a ludicrous idea.

Still, Belle had finished all the books Alvis had left her. Despite her malice towards where she was, the library had intrigued her. It had filled her with a thirst for knowledge and a sense of wonder that was burrowed deep inside of her. So, Belle decided to try. Even if it meant facing the beast.

Before leaving the room, a sudden fear took hold of her. With a shaking hand, she reached out and knocked on her bedroom wall three times.

Another request so soon? To what do I owe this pleasure?

"Where is Addy right now?"

I do not burden myself with such knowledge.

"Take a guess. Is she in the library?"

...No.

Belle felt the castle leave her mind. She shivered, smoothing down her dress before grabbing the books and opening the door. "Good enough for me."

She decided to walk with pure intention, straightening her back and lifting her chin high. Belle kept telling herself she was in control, and that no fear would bind her.
But, as her hands went to turn the doorknob of the library door, she heard voices from the other side.

Alvis. And Addy.

"Where is that botany book I had last week?"

"Over there. Has the castle decided to get creative again?"

"Yes, and I'd rather identify it sooner rather than later. I don't want to see Belle hurt. She doesn't have the luxury of being cursed. Or dead."

Belle's heart was in her throat. The castle had lied. She leaned closer to the door, continuing to listen. She could hear Alvis' voice getting closer.

"So you'll be in the garden all day then? Such a change to your normal routine."

She heard Addy laugh. "I do not appreciate- Alvis where are you going?"

At that moment, the library door swung open, causing Belle to stumble and take a step back. Alvis stood in the doorway, a wide grin on their spectral face.

"I thought I sensed somebody out here. Good morning, Miss Belle, what can I help you with?"

With her face burning with embarrassment, Belle sheepishly held up the pile of books. "I came to return these."

"Ah, wonderful! Step inside, would you? I loathe the idea of speaking in doorways."

They turned to walk back inside, gesturing with a wave of their fingers for Belle to follow. She stepped inside and followed Alvis to the table, veins frozen, wondering what would happen next. Addy stood on the other side, holding the large botany book in her huge hands.

Surprisingly, Addy smiled at Belle. It looked distorted on her face, but her yellow eyes flickered with an attempt of being genuine. If Addy could even be genuine. "Good morning."

She did not respond. Alvis noticed and glanced at Addy before turning their attention back to Belle. "Wonderful, how did you find them?"

Belle glanced at Addy out of the corner of her eye. She didn't react and simply watched the conversation while grazing a finger along the spine of the encyclopedia. She looked back at Alvis. "Not too bad. Different to what I used to read at home."

"Hm. What did you read at home?"

"A lot of old plays and fairy tales."

Alvis chuckled. "No wonder your head is filled with cautionary tales of magic. I'll expand your horizons Miss Belle don't you worry!"

They stepped up onto a set of ladders that was attached to one of the bookcases, climbing up to browse the shelves. Belle found herself once again looking for Addy's reaction. Waiting to see what the beast would do.

Addy noticed, and bowed her head to Belle, waving the book in her hand. "I think I'll take my leave. Try not to let Alvis give you too much to read in one go- they get excited."

"Hang on one moment Addy!" Alvis called from the ladder. "Do you still have that book?"

Addy had a strange look on her face, and tilted her head in confusion. "Alvis you're going to have to be more specific."

"The short one. With the caterpillar and the cat."

"Oh!" Addy seemed to have a moment of realisation. "Yes, I do."

"Are you finished with it?"

"Yes."

"Then why haven't you returned it?"

Belle watched as Addy's expression shifted to mild annoyance. "Because I'm re-reading it. It is a fascinating story."

Alvis kept one hand gripped on the ladder and turned back to Addy. "Why didn't you tell me you wanted to keep it for longer?"

"I didn't realise there was a time limit on reading books from a library in our home, Alvis."

"Yes, but it's still an inconvenience."

Addy stepped forward and point a finger at him. Belle stepped back, steering clear of Addy's figure. "YOU always said-,"

"Excuse me! Don't go pointing your claws at me, young lady." Alvis exclaimed, pointing a finger back.

Belle thought the two of them were about to fight, and this would descend into a screaming match. But when the two of them started laughing, it was obvious that Alvis was simply teasing Addy.

Addy let her hand drop to her side. "You are ridiculous when it comes to this library. I will take my leave now."

She walked to the door, and Alvis went back to the shelves, grabbing one of the books and climbing back down the ladder. "I want that book returned."

Addy looked over her shoulder. "Tomorrow. Have a pleasant day, you two."

She closed the door behind her. Belle stood, bewildered by the...domestic she had just witnessed. Alvis turned back to Belle, chuckling to themselves as they handed her the book. "She's so easy to tease sometimes."

"Has she...ever reacted badly to the teasing?" Belle asked, brushing a hand over the book cover and reading the title. It seemed to be a history book.

"Badly? No! Never. She's threatened to throw a book at me a few times, but has never actually followed through with it."

She raised an eyebrow. "Would it hit you though?"

"No," They replied, with another laugh. "It would go right through me. Now, let me see what else I have for you." Alvis started walking around the perimeter of the library, Belle trailing behind them as they kept adding books of all sizes to the pile in her hands. Every title was something different, something Belle would have never thought to have read before.

When Alvis could see Belle was struggling to carry the pile, they stopped. Belle went back to the table to put the stack down, opening the cover of the book at the top of the pile to skim through it.

"You've given me quite the variety here, Alvis."

"But of course. Books have infinite knowledge and infinite lessons we could learn. We should not let ourselves be scared of such power. Start with these, and let me know your thoughts."

"Thank you," Belle flicked through the pages. She stopped when she noticed one of the pages have a tear in the corner.

Alvis looked over her shoulder, wondering what she was reading. "Ah. Apologies for that. Took a lot of practice before Addy stopped ripping the pages entirely. If you find any that are unreadable, bring them back and I'll ask the castle to replace them."

"I see. It does not surprise me." Belle closed the book with a quick thud, not wanting to think of those wicked claws.

Alvis' hollow eyes glowed. "That comment was a little unnecessary Miss Belle."

Belle turned away. She braced herself for whatever nonsense she was going to be told about Addy. She had already come to her conclusions about the owner of the castle, and none of them were positive. Addy must have been cursed because of a price she refused to pay. A consequence she purposefully avoided. Somebody as reckless and selfish as that did not deserve even civility.

Alvis sighed. "You and Addy are adults and are perfectly capable of sorting this out yourselves. It's not my business."

She sighed in relief, almost smiling at them. "For once, I appreciate the lack of concern."

They laughed. Despite their appearance, their laugh was hearty and full of life. "I try not to worry about such trivial matters. But whatever does happen between the two of you, do not let fear be a factor in your decision."

"I thought you weren't going to comment on it?"

"That wasn't a comment, it was a philosophical perspective," Alvis explained, waving a hand to enunciate the point.

Belle picked up the pile of books, trying to hold them in one hand. "I suppose. I will get started on these, then."

"You can read in here if you want, or there's a lovely bench in the rose garden, or-,"

"I think I'll read in my room, for now."

Alvis nodded, bowing to Belle. "I understand. Let me get the door for you."

They did just that, ushering Belle out of the library. "Thank you." She said to them, trying to sound as genuine as she wanted to. "And thank you for not giving me a speech."

"Anytime, Miss Belle."

*****

That same night Belle returned to the library, a book in her hand. She had finished it before dinner and found it not to her liking. She slowly pushed open the library door and crept inside. She could hear the rain lashing outside, pounding against the windows. Thunder roared.
Belle turned to close the library door, behind her, and when she looked back into the library, a flash of thunder blasted through the windows, casting a demonic shadow across the room, complete with twisting horns that arched over the ceiling.

As she screamed, the demon stood up, exclaiming loudly across the room. "Spirits be damned!"

It was Addy, rising from her supposed usual reading spot. Belle clutched her chest with her free hand.

"You frightened me!" She snapped, speaking between panting breaths.

"I am so sorry, I didn't mean to." Addy kept her distance, holding her hands up.

Belle was ready to scream at her. She wanted to demand Addy drop the performance and act like the monster Belle knew she was inside.

"Forget it." She mumbled with a roll of her eyes. She held up the book so Addy could see it. "I came to return this."

"Oh!" Addy exclaimed, beginning the fidget with her claws.

"You can leave it on the table. I sent Alvis to bed. They were lingering around, and I wanted to read in peace."

Belle dropped the book on the table with a gentle thud. "I will take my leave, then."

"Wait!"

She tried not to groan as Addy turned around back to the window seat and began looking through the pile of books on there. She stepped towards Belle with a book in her hand, offering it to her.

"This is the book Alvis was asking me about this morning. The short one with the caterpillar and the rabbit. There's also a girl in a room of white·,"

"Leave it on the table." Belle quietly demanded, cutting her off. "Alvis can give it to me in the morning."

Addy complied, taking it over to the table as Belle turned to the door.

"Have I done something to upset you?"

Her question caused Belle to spin back around.

She continued, avoiding Belle's gaze. "I know I don't have much experience with people so I want to know if I've done something wrong."

Belle simply could not believe what she was hearing. "You expect me to not be upset that once again I have no control over my life? I was taken from my home, my family and forced to be stuck in a castle with something like you."

"There you go again," Addy's voice was quiet, her words hard like a rock. "Calling me something."

Belle's face twisted in disgust. "Am I meant to call you something else? A person?"

"Yes!" This was the first time Belle had heard Addy raise her voice, and it was terrifying. "I have tried to be nice to you. But you keep looking at me like that. Like I'm disgusting. I know I don't look like a woman, or sound like a woman, but under all this, I am a person!"

Belle stomped towards Addy, getting as close as her courage would allow her to. "The spirits may see you that way but I don't. I'm here because of you. Of your curses, your debts."

"You cannot simply walk in here like you know everything about me," Addy replied, her voice low, rumbling like the thunder outside. "I bow to the whims of the spirits, the same as you."

"And you must have done something truly horrible to have this fate. And now you have shared it with me."

Maybe Belle should have stopped here, should have ended the argument before she said something regretful. But she wanted to keep going. The anger was pushing her greed for answers. Addy, however, remained silent.

"You must have a wicked heart. You must, because no spirit would create something like this if there was not some malice in you."

Chapter 8

Please Don't Hurt Me
Adeline

Addy had never felt so disrespected in her entire life, both living years and cursed. Her still human heart shrivelled at Belle's every word. It was an emptiness she had never experienced.

She took a long breath, trying to compose herself before replying. But her words still came out brutal and sharp. "For goodness sake Belle. Get off the hill you're so desperate to die on!" Addy took a step back, trying to give herself some distance. "Has it ever occurred to you that this wickedness you speak of was not mine at all?"

Belle didn't respond. Addy looked down at her hands, at her disjointed fingers. The reminder of such wickedness. "We have something in common, at least. We are both here for someone else's mistake."

Belle scoffed. "At least my mistake came from a place of love. I cannot fathom the idea of someone loving you."

Addy felt like she had been stabbed, and look at Belle with horror in her eyes. It seemed Belle had the same expression, for as soon as those words left her lips, she marched out of the room, slamming the door behind her. Addy put her face in her hands and sank back into the window seat. If she could still cry, there would be tears down her face. Addy let out a loud sob that gripped her soul. The thunder roared outside, and after a while, Addy felt someone's presence beside her.

"Adeline?"

Wilmot's body was rising through the floor. As he came to his full height, Addy lifted her head. "How much did you hear?" She asked, her voice trembling.

"All of it. I came because I heard Belle scream, but...ended up hearing the rest." He put a hand on her shoulder. "Adeline..."

"I don't want to talk about it now."

"But‑,"

"Wil." She replied firmly. "I want to be left alone."

"Alright...you know where I am if you need me."

He vanished. Addy, with her soul now feeling lost to the void, curled up in the corner of the window seat and spent the night watching the storm.

*****

Addy didn't see Belle for another week.

However, the two ended up in each other's presence again, crossing paths between their usual times for breakfast. Addy, out of courtesy, now had her morning meal later than Belle, but it seemed on this day it had taken slightly longer for Belle to finish. Either that or Addy, for once, was early to something.

When the dining room door opened, Addy noticed Belle almost jump out of her chair in shock. Her cutlery clattered against the white plate, her teacup rattling in the patterned saucer. It was true that in the windowless dining room, a clawed hand latching over the door would frighten anyone, but Belle's reaction was still extreme.

Belle put a hand on the table, slowly rising out of her chair. Addy stepped away from the doorway, keeping to the opposite side of the room as Belle left without saying a word. When she had gone, Caris appeared, grabbing Belle's plate and cutlery She looked at Wilmot, who was standing near the kitchen door, and then back to Addy.

"Did something happen between you two? I haven't felt such a chill in a room since your parents were here."

Wilmot put a hand on Caris' arm as she made her way to the kitchen door. "Can you give me a moment to talk with Adeline alone, please?"

Caris turned back to Addy once more as if trying to read her expression. She nodded to Wilmot, albeit with great uncertainty. "I'll...occupy myself in the laundry room."

Once Caris had left the room, Addy took a seat on one of the many dining room tables, the skirt of her dress awkwardly moving around her knees as she sat on the seat. Wilmot took a seat next to her, folding his white misty fingers together.

"I'm surprised you haven't told Caris what you heard." She said as soon as he was seated.

Wilmot let out a loose breath akin to a laugh. "If I told Caris, she would have locked you two in a room until you were getting along again. Or she would have marched up to Belle and demanded she apologise. Alvis has a point, sometimes. You two are adults, and what happens next is up to you.”

“Then why are we having this conversation?” She asked, with a sigh as she tried to brush her hair back.

He paused. “Because words hurt, Adeline. I wanted to make sure you were alright.”

Despite how she was truly feeling, Addy chuckled, her throat suddenly dry. “Her words were cruel. But looking back, I think she just wanted someone to blame, and she could blame me.”

“So, you’re not upset at her?”

“I am upset, but I’m trying to see it from her perspective.” Addy shook her head. “I’m fine, Wil. I guess this is a part of the real world that I’m yet to understand.”

He nodded, putting a hand on her shoulder. “Sometimes, Adeline, we can’t make the world change for us. But, we can notice the parts we don’t like and know we can do better.”

Addy’s frown broke into a smile. “Wil, I think that is one of the most insightful things you’ve ever said.”

He made a face at her, scowling. “I’m turning into Alvis. My husband would be enraged if he was here. Right, enough of that then. I’ll get Caris to bring your breakfast.”

Chapter 9

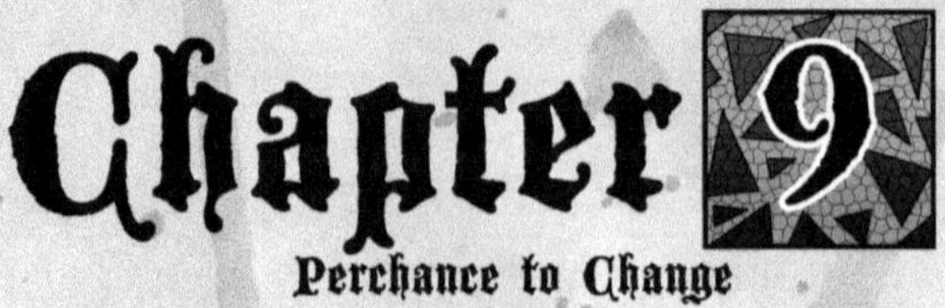

Perchance to Change
Bellerose

A month passed.

It surprised Belle how often time would move so swiftly. It seemed only a moment ago that she was running through the forest to get here. Time was often a trickster, allowing someone to think they have control of it. Despite herself, Belle had gotten used to the daily routine of the castle and the beings who lived there.

Belle and Addy had not spoken a word to each other. And Belle preferred it that way. A part of her regretted some of the words she said, but the sentiment still rang true in Belle's mind. Maybe, if this was any other situation, she would feel some remorse for Addy. But she couldn't bring herself to do it. Not here, not now. Not yet.

Although she hated to admit it, she took it too far.

She would keep to herself during her time here, and hopefully, Addy would do the same.

One morning, not long after breakfast, however, Belle heard voices coming from one of the staircases tucked away from the castle foyer. It was Addy's voice and another that she did not recognise.

As Belle turned the corner, she found Addy sitting on the stairs, talking to a spirit dressed as a pirate.

Of all the things Belle thought she would find in this castle, this was the last thing she expected.

Although he lacked a defined physical form, the pirate spirit still had an iconic tricorn hat and long coat, with many brass buttons. He sported a braided beard and a scar over his right eye.

"That's when I saw it- the Kraken leapt out of the ocean right at these sailors!"

Then Addy *gasped*. Like a child hearing a bedtime story.

"No! What did they do?"

"The captain, the fool that he was, told the men to grab the harpoons!" The pirate spirit swung his arm up into the air like he was holding the harpoon himself. "But of course, the harpoons-,"

"Wait, wait, stop for a moment." Addy held up her hands to him. "What's a harpoon again?"

The pirate spirit stepped back, miming the shape of the harpoon with his hands. "It's almost like a long spear that-,"

But then the spirit noticed Belle watching them. "Addy, you didn't tell me you had a guest!"

Addy leaned forward, her eyes meeting Belle's. "Belle?" Awkwardly, Belle stepped towards the two of them from around the corner. "I will take my leave."

"No!" Addy shook her head, flustering as she waved her hands. "Wait a moment. At least let me introduce you."

Addy gestured to the spirit, and then back to Belle. "Belle, meet Captain Barnaby. Barnaby, this is Belle. She's...staying with us for a while. It's a bit of a long story."

Barnaby stuck out a ghostly hand to Belle. "Aye, I see! A pleasure to meet you, miss. Would you care to join us?"

Belle didn't take his hand. As much as she wanted to leave, what she had heard had piqued her interest. "What exactly are you two doing?"

Barnaby didn't let Belle's impoliteness bother him. He dropped his hand and immediately grinned. "I'm catching Addy up on my adventures in the Eastern seas!"

Addy clapped her hands together, almost as if she had forgotten their confrontation a month ago. "Barnaby wanders along the seas, hopping on boats and joining the crew on voyages. He comes here every month to tell me the stories."

"Yes! Exactly! Can't let you miss out on all the fun of the sea."

Addy gestured to the other side of the step she was sitting on. "Please, join us."

She wanted to refuse, but the idea of such a story interested her. What did Belle have to lose? She took a seat a few steps upwards, keeping her distance from Addy. She smoothed out the creases of her lilac skirt and put her hands in her lap. "Where are we in the story?"

Addy turned to Belle, reaching up to move a strand of hair behind her horns. "The sailors got attacked by a Kraken."

Belle raised an eyebrow. "A Kraken? What's a Kraken?"

"A giant squid-like monster, miss," Barnaby explained. "Huge creature!"

"And the sailors were going to use harpoons," Addy added, waving with her hand to encourage Barnaby to continue.

"Harpoons- yes harpoons!" Barnaby took the cue. "That was where we were. So the sailors took the harpoons, they're big spears, and threw them into the water."

Barnaby's story went on for another hour. Although Belle was trying to show little reaction to the current situation she found herself in, even she couldn't resist getting excited as Barnaby told his tale. The pirate spirit had a penchant for performance, and it was...almost amusing for both herself and Addy to turn into active spectators. Addy interrupted every so often to ask questions, allowing Belle to avoid the awkwardness of interrupting herself. The story ended with the entire boat barely surviving the attack and making it safely back to shore. A little bit less dramatic than Belle would have expected, but still wholly enjoyable.

Barnaby, looking pleased with himself for having more than one listener to his story time, put his hands on his hips, even though he did not have hips. He spoke to Addy with a wide grin. "Same time next month?"

Addy beamed. "Most certainly."

He looked to Belle expectantly. "Will you join next time as well Miss Belle?"

She smiled, nodding with more enthusiasm than she thought she would. "I would like that if you wouldn't mind Captain."

"The more the merrier. Now, I must be off. I hear there's a ship leaving for undiscovered lands. So I will bid you adieu, Adeline." He bowed to Addy. "And to you Belle." He bowed to Belle and vanished in a swirl of smoke.

When he was going, Addy laughed aloud. "I suppose you would not have expected that this morning, hm?"

Belle looked to where Barnaby had once been. "I thought it was only the four of you who were here."

"It's five if you count the castle." Addy shrugged, looking down to mess with the hem of her dress.

Belle stood up, dusting off her skirt. She nodded to Addy. "Thank you for allowing me to join you. I will take my leave."

As she went to turn away, Addy stretched out her arm to her. "Wait!"

Belle pivoted back around, but the sight of Addy's hand made her flinch. She must have seen the reaction in Belle's hand, as Addy lowered her arm.

"Barnaby comes here every month, as I said before. Same time, usually the same place." Addy explained, looking down as she brought her hands back to her lap. "We get other visitors here too...Cornelius likes to talk a lot about the Wild Hunt if you're interested. He pops into the library now and then to talk through where he's spotted them. And Malcolm is a little creepy talking about the cemetery he worked at but it's endearing. Oh, and if Gertrude asks to talk about cabbages, you can say no. We've been encouraging her to respect boundaries."

Belle listened to Addy's ramble as she talked openly about every spirit who wandered into the castle. She wondered how she could be so...calm? Had she resigned herself to her fate over the mistakes she had made, or was she so ignorant that she lived on in deceitful bliss?

"You're being nice again."

Addy looked at Belle, confused. "Would you prefer it if I wasn't?"

Belle huffed. "I was expecting different after our...disagreement."

She almost laughed in response, her yellow eyes glinting in an almost mischievous way. "What, were you expecting broken furniture? A castle in ruins? A beast with a temper? Forgive me for not living up to expectations Belle, I was raised better than that."

"So, you're simply going to continue to act like this situation is normal?"

Addy shrugged. "At the end of the day, Belle, you're still a guest in my home. What you said to me was horrifically cruel, entirely unnecessary and incredibly degrading. But I still wish to offer you a basic level of respect, even if you do not return it."

Belle grew tired of Addy's insistent attempts to act like a human. However, as much she hated to admit it, Addy's words had truth to them. She could have walked away there and then, maybe even mumbling a vague but genuine apology.

But Belle's curiosity was a deadly weapon.

She wanted answers.

"Was this your fault?"

She blinked in surprise. "I'm sorry?"

"This." Belle waved a hand towards Addy. "Your curse. You said the last time we spoke that this was someone else's wickedness. So answer me this, Addy. Did you not pay a debt? Is this your consequence for not paying the price?"

Addy was quiet for a moment. She grabbed the handrail and stood up, lifting her head to Belle. There was a deep sadness in her voice. "I *was* the price."

Belle's mouth opened in shock, and her eyes were wide. For once, Belle didn't have the words.

So, Addy continued. "This...situation is because of a debt that wasn't mine, that I'm now paying. That is why I said we had something in common."

She felt unsteady on her feet. If Addy was telling the truth, then Belle had made all the wrong assumptions.

"This wasn't your fault?"

Addy tried to laugh, but it was an empty one, so different from the one she shared with Barnaby. "No, I was a child when this happened. Even back then I knew better than to make debts I couldn't pay."

Another silence settled back between them. Then, Addy broke it. "Did you expect it to have been my debt?"

"I..." There was no denying it now. "Yes. I thought you had done some horrible thing to have caused such a consequence."

Addy gave her a half-smile. "I am not surprised. I admit now the impression I gave when we first met was not a positive one."

"Oh?"

She sighed. "When we first met, I was having a particularly bad day. You remember Wilmot mentioning I had been unwell?"

Belle nodded. Addy continued, now leaning against the handrail. "It happens sometimes. Everything hurts, I'm unsure whether it's part of the curse or...maybe the despair gets to me sometimes. Regardless it leaves me in a foul mood. Now, I know that is not an excuse for my behaviour towards you, so I want to apologise. I never wanted to question your morals or speak ill of your father. From my brief interaction with him, it was clear he cared for you."

Belle bit her lip and wiped her eyes to avoid the tears that formed from falling down her face. She hadn't heard someone speak of her family for a while now, and she still missed them every day.

She swallowed, giving Addy a firm nod. "I appreciate the apology, and I understand. And I accept the fact I made some harsh judgements."

Addy stood upright, holding her skirt in one hand. "Fear does make us say wild things, doesn't it?" She replied, chuckling and shaking her head. "Enjoy the rest of your day."

Belle remained still as Addy walked up the stairs, disappearing down the hallway. She sat back down on the step, burying her head in her hands. How could she have been so ridiculous?

She should have asked the question sooner and avoided all the anguish. Belle realised that she was just the same back home. Always finding the worst outcomes and people and their situations. Maybe that was why she was so firm in her refusal of Thomas, of rejecting her sister's ideals surrounding happiness in life. When confronted with something new, Belle was hungry for answers, for opinions.

Greed to know all and know it all.

Maybe now, for the time she was here, she could learn to tolerate the beast known as Adeline. It was a start towards the concept known as civility.

Chapter 10

Thorns

Adeline

Addy pulled at one of the decaying branches from the rose bush, freeing it from the bundle of blooms and leaves. She never minded the feeling of the thorns when she was young, but now she felt nothing because of the tree bark that had grown over her skin. It was tough, like old earth and bones.

She enjoyed tending to the roses, her one selfish request from the castle. It had flourished through her decade of tending to it, a bouquet of different colours and varieties. Some grew in bushes along the ground, some along the stone walls that surrounded the garden. Some had even crept up the old fountain that had long stopped working.

It was a delightful display, and even on her worst days, Addy could not limit her love for it. She wiped the dirt onto her already messy skirt and let out a sharp breath to blow a strand of hair out of her face.

Caris would throw a fit later over the state of her. But right now, Addy was breathing in the sunshine, and the smell of the roses.

For a moment, everything was normal.

She heard footsteps on the flagstone path, the sound of loose pebbles skittering away. Turning her head, she saw Belle standing at the archway which served as the garden's entrance.

Addy went still, waiting to see what Belle would do. Whether she would immediately turn away, or at least try and talk to her.

"This must be where my father got the rose from, am I correct?" She asked, different to her usual way of greeting her.

Addy nodded, wiping some loose dirt from her palms. Belle continued, stepping into the threshold of the garden. "Is this your garden?"

"I like to think so. Though it was from the castle, so I suppose it is technically the owner. But I look after it."

"It's..." Belle took a breath. "It's impressive."

Addy blinked in surprise over what seemed to be a compliment from Belle. She carefully got to her feet, making sure not to trip over her skirt. "That is a kind thing for you to say."

Belle didn't reply, only continuing to look around the garden, and admiring the roses. However, when she moved her hands, Addy noticed something that made her heart drop with worry.

"You're hurt." She blurted out.

Belle lifted her arm slightly, revealing several cuts across her arm. There were light spots of blood. She immediately covered it with her hand. "It's nothing, I caught my arm on something."

"Let me see." Addy passively demanded, taking a step forward.

Belle instantly took a step back. Addy took a long breath, wondering how to approach this. "Please, I'm not going to hurt you. I want to make sure you're okay."

Her tone was flat. "Why?"

"Because I haven't quite worked out every plant that grows in this garden yet, and to be quite frank Belle I don't want to see you hurt, or worse, dead."

The two of them kept their stance for a long time. Addy kept her hand outstretched. It seemed like Belle was thinking it all through, and Addy couldn't tell which way this was going to go.

But before either of them could work it out, Belle stumbled as she stood. Addy lunged forward, catching her as she fell forward. "Belle!?"

Addy held Belle awkwardly in her arms as she knelt on the floor. She tried to wake her up, but nothing was working. She banged on the ground three times, and before the castle could say anything, she made her demands.

"Get Caris. Please get Caris!"

*****

It had taken Caris, Wilmot and Addy to get Belle back to her bedroom and into her bed. She was now lying under the bedsheets, as Addy held a cold compress to her head while sat on the edge of the bed. It was the closest she had ever been to Belle since she first arrived.

Addy snapped her head to the door as Caris opened it, carrying a handful of medical supplies, ranging from bandages to ointments.

Caris hurried over to the bedside, and Addy move down the bed to let her work. "The castle is being deliberately vague over what plant Belle cut herself on. Perhaps it feels bad. Still, Alvis is working on some medicine."

"Will...will she be okay?" Addy asked, her voice trembling as she watched Belle sleep.

"Yes. She'll be fine in a few days." Caris said, and they both breathed a sigh of relief.

"This is my fault," Addy said after a moment of quiet. "If I had been able to identify the rest of the plants‧,"

"You cannot blame yourself," Caris said, turning back to put a hand to Addy's face. "Nobody could have predicted something like this."

Addy looked past Caris, and to Belle once more. Despite all that had been said between them, the last thing Addy wanted was to see her suffer. Caris kept her hand on Addy's face. "You can rest, I'll take care of her."

"No," Addy stated, continuing to look at Belle. "I won't be able to do anything until she's awake. Let me stay with you."

Caris smiled, letting go of Addy's face and turning back to Belle. "As you wish."

Chapter 11

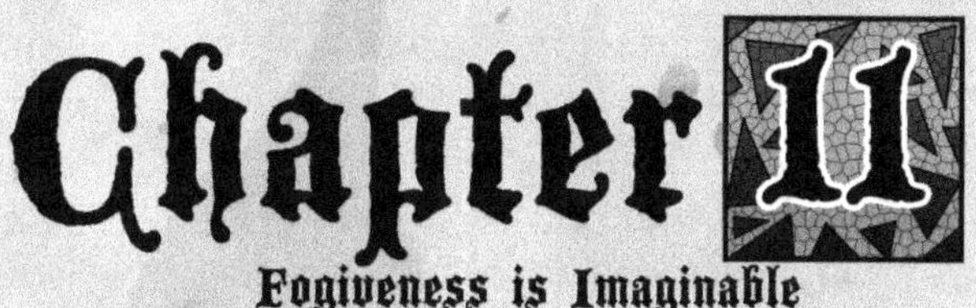

Fogiveness is Imaginable

Bellerose

Belle's eyes slowly opened. To her surprise, she wasn't in the garden. To her further surprise, she was in her bedroom, with Caris and Addy standing over her, with looks of pure joy on their faces.

"Spirits be damned!" Caris exclaimed, immediately going over to the bedroom wall and knocking on it three times.

"Tell Wilmot and Alvis that Miss Belle is awake...don't you start, we'll discuss your botany habits later."

Addy was sat on the end of the bed, hands folded together in her lap. "You had us worried, how are you feeling?"

"What..." Belle lifted her head and tried to look around. "What happened?"

Before Addy could respond, Caris thrust a bowl into her hands. "Go get some fresh water, please."

Addy hesitated, so Caris began shooing her out of the room. "Water, Addy. Now!"

Reluctantly, Addy left the room. When she was gone, Caris adjusted Belle's pillows and helped her to sit up. "You passed out in the garden," Caris explained, immediately answering the questions Belle was going to ask. "Addy summoned us and we brought you here.

We think you had an adverse reaction to something, but the castle is vague on the details."

"Addy...Addy was there when I fainted? I remember speaking to her but..."

"She has not left your side," Caris stated with a firm nod. "She felt a lot of guilt over this."

Belle was struggling to process what Caris was saying. Why would Addy want to stay by her side, after everything Belle had said to her? Such animosity must have created a rift between them, so why was Addy so concerned for her life?

The door opened, and Addy returned with a fresh bowl of water and a clean cloth. She stood awkwardly in the doorway, her figure taking up most of the space.

"Um, Caris? Alvis needs you."

"Did they say why?"

Addy shook her head. "They just asked me to get you."

Caris sighed, standing up. "Alright. You're not out of the woods yet Belle, you still need to rest, so don't think about moving. Now, be civil to each other. I'll be back soon."

She left the room, and Addy walked over to the bed, putting down the bowl on the side table and sitting on the wooden stool Caris had been sitting on. "Can I change your compress? Or would you like to do it yourself?" Addy asked, grabbing the clean cloth.

Belle glanced over at her. "Have you been here the entire time I was passed out?"

Addy blinked a few times, processing the question. "Yes."

She met Addy's gaze. Even though her eyes were intense, Belle could see there was now a softness to them. "Thank you."

Addy smiled at her. "You're welcome. Now, compress?"

Belle tried to will her body to move, but even the days of rest had left her lethargic. Addy seemed to understand, even though no words were said, and stood up. She peeled off the old compress and used it to brush away the strands of hair on Belle's forehead and over her eyes. Every move was with a gentle caution, it was clear Addy was trying to not catch Belle's skin with her claws. She lay the new compress on Belle's forehead and sat back down.

"Do you need anything?"

Belle could feel her eyelids drooping, and she held back a yawn. "I want to sleep again."

She chuckled. "Then sleep. I'll keep an eye on you until Caris is back."

As Belle closed her eyes, it made her realise that Addy's actions here were human kindness, not akin to a beast at all, and sleep found her quickly.

Chapter 12
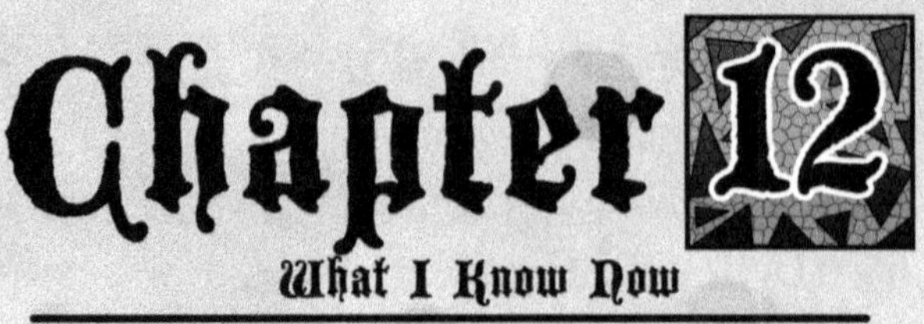

What I Know Now
Adeline

In a shocking twist, Belle had allowed Addy to continue to visit while she finished recovering. The visits were short and brief, mostly to change a compress or check the bandages when Caris was busy with something else. Wilmot and Alvis had already checked in as well, dropping off books and food when it was requested.

Addy carefully made her way to Belle's bedroom door, clean bandages and medicine in hand. The cut on Belle's arm continued to heal nicely, but it needed to be checked regularly. She reached up a hand and knocked on the door, though it sounded more like a rough bang. That didn't seem to matter though, as it appeared Belle recognised who it was.

"You can come in Addy."

Addy pushed open the door, clumsily making her way to Belle's bedside and putting down the bandages and medicine on the side table. "How are you doing?" She asked as she sat down on the stool.

"Much better," Belle said. It was true, the colour was back in her freckled cheeks. She was no longer wearing the compress, and according to the spirits, was eating the meals she was given. "Caris says I should be out of bed by tomorrow."

"That's wonderful news," Addy replied, genuinely happy to see her having made such a recovery. "Do you mind if I check the cut again?"

Belle held out her arm. "I know what you're going to say."

"And what's that?" She asked.

"This is going to sting a little," Belle replied, with a wry smile. "But it helps keep the cut clean."

Addy laughed at her sarcasm, and grabbed the cloth, pouring the ointment onto it. She dabbed the cloth onto the cut, and Belle held back a wince. Addy couldn't help but chuckle a little at Belle's attempts to be brave. She met her gaze as she continued to work. "I hope this hasn't put you off exploring the gardens."

Belle rolled her eyes. "No, but it is more dangerous than I thought."

"You went through a whole forest to get here," Addy replied, raising an eyebrow.

"Yes, but there was a road I could follow. There are no gardens like this in Reverie."

"Is that where you're from?" Addy tried to think if she had seen the name on any maps. "What is it like?"

"It is a farming town. So no forests, or rose gardens, but lots of wheat fields. Then a nice little town that's nestled between all of it."

"It sounds wonderful. Do you like living there?"

"I do. For the most part."

Addy put the cloth down and grabbed the bandages. They were making small talk. That wasn't leading to an insult. "For the most part?"

"It's the same with most towns. It's small. My father is a merchant and would go to the port towns and see so many wonderful things. Home feels so limiting once you know there's more."

"I know that feeling." Addy started to gently wrap the bandage around her arm. "Do you have four siblings, by the way?"

Belle looked surprised. "How did you guess?"

Addy chuckled. "Caris and I play this game and have done it since I was a child. We guess people's stories. I guessed your father had five children at home. So, that's you and four siblings."

"Quite the observation. But yes, I have two sisters and two brothers."

"Well, I'm happy I guessed right." She tied off the bandage and waved her hand over it with a flourish. "There! It's close to being fully healed, but I'd rather keep the dirt out of it for now."

Belle looked like she wanted to say something to her. As she shifted in the bed to sit up straighter, she did say it. "Can I play the game? Can I guess your story?"

Addy was suddenly curious. "If you want to, yes."

Belle bit her lip, turning her head away for a brief moment, before meeting Addy's eyes. "I think I was wrong about you. About who you are."

Addy felt her heart burning through her chest.

"And I am sorry for how I've been acting. I made a judgement about you based on my fears, without giving you a chance. I was incredibly cruel to you, and despite all that, you still chose to treat me with kindness and respect that I didn't deserve. I am truly sorry for what I said that night, Addy. And I'm sorry it took me this long to realise how wrong I was."

It felt like time had frozen for her. Addy processed what Belle was saying, trying to discern how much of it had truly come from the heart. Addy knew that this forgiveness was not a one-way road and that she was also at fault.

"I truly appreciate the apology. I am sorry again for how I spoke about your father and for how harsh I was that night as well."

Belle put her hand on Addy's arm. Addy felt her heart skip several beats at that moment, a strange new feeling taking over. It felt like roses.

"Thank you for taking care of me."

Addy put her hand over Belle's and saw her eyes widen at the gesture. "I couldn't have you dying to a plant under my care, now could I?"

Chapter 13

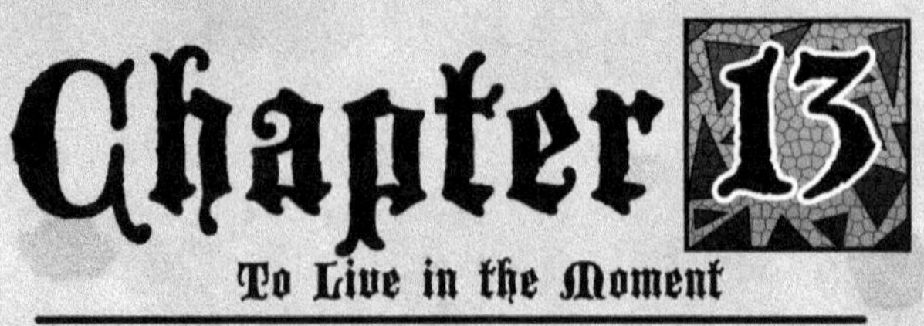

To Live in the Moment

Bellerose

Belle kept fiddling with the bandage on her arm as she walked through the garden, something she had started doing daily. There was something new in the air since Belle and Addy had apologised to each other. Since Belle stopped letting her fear control her, it opened up the chance to get to know Addy for the person she was on the inside. They had been having actual conversations since Belle was able to be out of bed. Granted, they were still short and sweet, but often delved past the typical greetings and questions of well-being.

It all linked back to what Caris had told her. To be kind to Addy.

All this time, Addy had been kind to her, and Belle let her own prejudices cloud her opinion. Perhaps it was time to return the favour.

The moment to do just that presented itself, as when Belle turned the corner on her usual path, she found Addy crouching down over a plant that was growing not far from one of the stones. Mud *covered* the hem of the green she wore. Her hair had fallen in front of her face, and she kept tucking it behind her ear. There was an open blank book in her hand, and an open book on the floor, which appeared to be about botany.

Something spurned Belle to walk towards her, and not run away this time. She called out to Addy. "What are you doing?"

"Ah!" Addy cried out, falling backwards onto the path. The book flew out of her hands. Belle covered her mouth, gasping, and rushed over. Addy looked up and realised who was standing over her. "Belle?"

She started to shake her head, muttering apologies to Addy. "I didn't mean to startle you."

Addy outstretched a hand and grabbed her book, which was now covered in a light dust of dirt. She gave it a good shake, cleaning out the pages. "No harm done." She explained with a smile. "Just a surprise."

Belle almost laughed. The beast, as she had known Addy for so long, was easily startled by a rogue voice in the garden. She had noticed all the times before when Addy rambled for too long or stumbled as she lost her footing. They were human qualities that Belle did not see before.
She, not even thinking, held out a hand to Addy. "Here, let me help you up."

Addy hesitated for a moment before taking Belle's hand, and getting to her feet in an unsteady manner. As the two of them stood facing each other, hands still locked around one another, their eyes met. Belle felt her stomach churn, not from fear, but from something else entirely.

Instantly, she let go of Addy's hand and gathered the two books that were on the floor, offering them back to Addy.
She took them, and Belle decided to take a look at the

plant she was studying. "Is this something the castle has grown?"

Addy didn't respond right away. It was almost like the interaction had left her in a daze. She seemed to snap out of it, looking at the plant as well. "Yes! I think it might be wormwood." She opened the botany book, flicking through it before showing Belle the page with the entry on it. "See? The leaves look similar. But also it has another name, mugwort."

Belle looked at the page, and back at the herb. "Odd place to plant a herb. Do you not have a herb garden?"

Addy rolled her eyes, the sharp green colour shimmering in the sunlight. "One would think it's that simple. But no, the castle likes to experiment. Anyway...mugwort has a lot more names, like the felon herb, naughty man, old man, and St John's plant, but that's different from St John's wort and...I'm rambling."

Belle chuckled. "Yes, you're rambling. Is mugwort safe?"

Addy's eyes narrowed as she read the page. She nodded. "It's fine."

She took her blank notebook and grabbed the ink pen that she had tied to it with a loose bit of string. Addy made a quick note that simply read: *Mugwort- safe.*

She closed the books, tucking them both under her arm. Belle took a deep breath. "Are you going to try and see what other plants there are?"

"Yes," Addy replied, with a huge smile on her face. "I think there might be something new at the edges of the garden. I want to take a look."

"Can I come with you?"

Addy went still, turning slowly to look at Belle as her smile wavered. "You want to come with me?"

"Yes."

"You want to catalogue plants...with me?"

"Yes," Belle let out a light laugh. "That's why I asked."

"You want to willingly spend time with me?"

Belle stuttered, and she felt suddenly under pressure. "Y-yes."

"Cataloguing plants? With me?"

"Yes, Addy! Yes, I want to catalogue plants with you." She replied, exasperated.

Addy's face softened, and her voice was quiet like a mouse. She sounded so timid. "*Really?*"

"Yes. I am not doing this in jest I would genuinely like to take a walk around the garden with you."

She looked as if she was going to break with joy as her smile returned. Addy turned around on one foot, her voice full of glee. "I would love that. Alright, let us go. Let me lead the way."

Belle couldn't help but share Addy's newfound light. "Naturally, and I will follow."

*****

It was well into the afternoon by the time Belle and Addy had finished taking a tour of the garden. Together, they had identified twelve new kinds of plants, as well as making casual conversation in between. Addy had spent a lot of time spewing off random facts to Belle, but she didn't complain. She had never met someone who spoke with such passion as Addy did. Nobody in Reverie could ever compare to Addy's enthusiasm for plant life.

They reached one of the back doors that led back into the castle, and the two stopped to take a breath. Belle looked down, and her eyes were wide when she realised now both of their dress hems were covered in mud.

"My goodness, we're filthy."

Addy laughed. "Yes, that is obvious."

Belle picked up a part of her skirt, holding it out. "This would probably come out if I washed it. Yours too."

Addy also picked up her skirt. "I don't know how I would do that."

"You..." Belle's mouth dropped. "You were never taught how to wash clothes?"

"Um..." Addy stuttered. "No, not really."

"Did the spirits not think to teach you that?"

"It never came up. Caris takes charge of that kind of thing."

"Addy· oh my goodness." Belle put a hand to her cheek. "Do you get your water from the well we passed?"

"Y·yes."

"Right. Let us both go and get changed, and I will meet you back there. Bring your dress with you."

Addy laughed in disbelief. "Why, what are you going to do?"

"In exchange for all of the facts I've learned about plants today, I will teach you how to wash your clothes."

"Are you sure that's a good idea?" She questioned, raising a clawed hand to Belle.

"No excuses! Go get changed, I will see you in a while."

*****

Before heading back out to the well, Belle stopped in the kitchen, trying to see if she could find where the laundry items were kept. She had gotten changed into a dark blue dress with white flowers on the sleeves, which wasn't usually her colour. She started going through the cupboards, muttering to herself as she held her dirty dress in one hand.

"Are you looking for something, dear?"

Belle lifted her head out from the cupboards and saw Caris standing on the other side of the room.

She nodded to the spirit. "I was looking for where you keep the brushes and soap for the laundry?"

Caris looked puzzled. "If you need something cleaned, I can handle it."

"Oh- no, it's okay. I offered to teach Addy how to wash her clothes."

She blinked a few times in surprise. "Ah, I see."

Belle was self-conscious all of a sudden, clutching the dress in her hand. "If that's okay, of course. It was simply that Addy mentioned she didn't know how, and we've spent the day in the garden so I offered-,"

"You two spent the day together?" Caris asked, interrupting Belle's explanation.

Belle nodded, biting her lip. "Yes."

Caris's smile returned. "So that's where you two have been. I was wondering where you were hiding." She disappeared into one of the side doors, returning with a bucket, a brush, soap and wooden pegs. She tilted her head towards the door she just came out of. "Bring them there when you're done, there's a place to hang them out to dry."

"Of course. Thank you, Caris."

She bowed her head. "A pleasure, I hope the lesson goes well."

*****

Belle did have doubts as to whether Addy would return to meet her at the well. Sure enough though, Addy was there waiting on the stone bench that had been set nearby, mud-covered dress in hand. What also surprised Belle was that she and Addy were now wearing dresses of the same colour.

When she spotted Belle, Addy stood up, walking over to take the buckets from her hand. She looked Belle up and down, smirking. "Hm. We both have great taste, it seems. The colour suits you."

Belle felt like her insides twisted, and she could feel herself burning up. She gave her head a light shake, dismissing the feeling, and sat down on the bench. Addy was already taking the step and filling the bucket up with water from the well. When she sat back down, Belle ran through the steps on how to use the soap and brush.

Turns out, despite having literal claws, Addy was a natural.

The two cleaned in silence for the first few minutes. Belle kept looking over at Addy to check on her progress. She was surprised at how much effort Addy was putting into this.

"You know," She said as she got up to empty her bucket of dirty water onto some bushes nearby. "My sisters have never done this in their life."

"Really?" Addy stopped scrubbing, giving her hand a moment of rest. "How come?"

"Oh, Mira and Clara would always say their hands were too delicate for such work," Belle explained.

As Addy lifted the dress out of the water, Belle offered her the bucket with clean water inside. She began to repeat the process and emptying the bucket and refilling it.

Addy went back to scrubbing. "So you always did this by yourself? What about your brothers?"

Belle shook her head, sitting back down and dunking her dress into the clean water. "Eder and Faron were never one for domestic chores. It was mostly left to me."

"Is this what your life is? Taking care of your home and your family?" Addy's eyes softened as she spoke.

Belle thought that she felt sorry for her. She thought for a moment, letting out a tight breath. "It's complicated. Yes, I would take care of everyone, but I had a job. At the town library actually."

Addy smiled. "That sounds wonderful. I am sorry that the debt took you away from that."

"I had lost the job before I came here," Belle said, bitterness in her voice. It had been half a year since that day, and she was still scorned by the events of it.

"What happened?" She asked, putting down the brush next to her. "If you don't mind me asking, that is."

Belle copied her and put her hands in her lap. "It turned out that...the intention with that job was to get me to marry the librarian's son, Thomas."

Addy didn't reply right away. It was clear she was absorbing what Belle had said. When she did speak, it was with a gentle softness. "I'm guessing you didn't want to marry him?"

"No? Well, I didn't love him. And I wasn't going to marry someone I didn't love. But it was also the principle of it."

"What do you mean?"

"I…" Belle took a long and deep breath, trying to make sense of what she was going to say. "I never liked the idea of doing what I was told I should do. My sisters loved the idea of getting married and settling down but that always felt weird to me. Is it wrong to think that? I've been so clouded by what I've been told. I have been made into the image of what is desired for me, not what I am. When I do go home, can I even go back to the part I was playing before?"

Addy rested her hands on the bench, leaning back on them. She looked up at the sky, as it brought in the evening.

"Alvis and I once discussed fate, and the idea that something is guiding us, beyond the spirits. We both agreed that everything happens for a reason. Whether good, bad or in my case, cursed, there is a reason. Perhaps it is the same for you. You had to leave your home and your family to come here, may be the start of something new for you. When the castle has said you have paid your debt, you can begin again. Build something new for yourself, changed by your experience here."

"Do you think I can do that?" Belle asked, lifting her head to watch the same sky as her Without realising, her fingers had overlapped with Addy's. "Finally take control again?"

"If you could look past your judgement to see me as I am, anything is possible," Addy answered, a bright smile returning to her face.

The two lowered their heads, and Belle looked down at their now intertwined fingers. Belle let out a yelp of surprise, pulling her hand away. "Oh my goodness I am so sorry!"

Addy lifted her hand off the bench. "No, no! It's fine! I am so sorry I didn't realise."

"It was my fault, really I…" Belle was gripping her hands together, feeling her face go pink. "I realised we had a very personal discussion and…"

Addy let out a laugh, seeming to be embarrassed as well, even if she couldn't blush. "You do not need to apologise. This is the longest we've ever spoken and to be quite honest, it felt wonderful."

Belle was stunned into silence. Addy, clearly not wanting to be the awkward one for once, started wringing out the dresses and throwing away the water once more. She stood up, tidying everything up and grabbing the stacked buckets with both hands. "I'll take these back to the kitchen and hang them up. I know where Caris usually takes them."

"I don't mind doing that." Belle offered, holding her hands out.

Addy shook her head. "It's fine, I know you have dinner first so you should get ready for that."

Belle suddenly realised that she didn't want to stop talking to Addy. Something was stirring inside of her, a feeling that she couldn't explain.

Perhaps this was what Addy was talking about. Was this how to begin again?

"Actually-," Belle got up from the bench and stood next to Addy. "Would you like to have dinner together tonight?"

Addy's eyes widened. Belle hadn't noticed it until now, but her eyes glimmered as if they were gold coins. The buckets almost fell from Addy's hands. "I would love that."

*****

That evening, two places were set at the dinner table, albeit still on opposite sides.

They both started to eat, the two of them trying to carry on a conversation with the distance between them.

Halfway through the meal, Addy put down her fork. Belle looked over, narrowing her eyes to see what was going on. "I now realise how incredibly awkward this must have been when you first arrived."

Belle put down her fork as well, pushing out her chair and standing up. "This will not do." She grabbed her plate and cutlery.

"What are you doing?" Addy asked.

Belle walked down to Addy, putting her plate down on the seat next to hers. She went back to grab her glass and napkin as well, before returning to take a seat in the chair next to Addy.

Addy looked alarmed. Belle realised that they were barely inches away from each other. She swallowed the feeling and picked up her fork once more. "Much better, now we can have a proper conversation."

Addy giggled. "I admit, I much prefer this. What were you saying before?"

"Oh?" Belle thought for a moment. "Ah, yes. Have you ever seen the ocean?"

She shook her head at Belle, talking in-between bites of food. "No, I didn't get a chance to see it before I was cursed."

"Hm." Belle tapped her fork against her plate. "That's a shame. My father has always described it to me. It sounds beautiful."

"Maybe one day we can go," Addy replied, her voice quiet.

Belle picked up her glass, raising it to Addy. "It's a promise. Once all debts are paid."

Addy raised her glass and clinked it with Belle's. "Once all debts are paid."

"Is everything alright in here?"

Belle turned and screamed at the sight of Wilmot's head poking through the door to the kitchen. Addy turned around, looking over the back of her chair. Her horns made a sharp sound as they scratched the wood. "I told you that would freak her out!"

Belle was still staring at Wilmot's head. "Spirits can do that?"

Wilmot smiled. "We can do a lot of things, Miss Belle. Surely you realise that by now. Anyway, do you two need anything?"

Addy sighed. "No, Wil, we're all well here. Thank you, though."

Wilmot disappeared back through the door, his voice echoing. "Let us know if you need us!"

Addy and Belle both turned back to their food. Belle's eyes wandered up to Addy's horns, and down to her arms and hands. "I understand if this is too personal a question but is your cursed body simply an appearance thing or…?"

Addy thought for a moment, resting her chin on her hand. "It's hard to explain, perhaps both? It's hard to walk sometimes, as you know. My skin is tough and cracked. I spent ages scratching everything with my fingers. The horns get in the way, I bang them on everything and it makes my hair hard to manage. Overall it is a bit inconvenient."

She finished her long ramble with a laugh as if used to the tedious nature of her life. Belle put down her cutlery again and crossed her arms, leaning forward on the table. "I think the fact that you still find the strength to carry on through all of that is admirable."

Addy smiled lightly. "It's all I've ever known. What else can I do, if not keep fighting?"

"Do you not remember your childhood before you were cursed?"

She waved a hand dismissively. "It's all hazy. The moment I was cursed is something I remember. That's always clear."

Belle nodded. She understood why Addy would be reluctant to relive such trauma. "Do Alvis, Wilmot and Caris know about that day?"

"They were there. Though I didn't know it at the time. We've never talked about it though. When I'm ready, I'll talk about it." Addy spoke with admirable determination. "But not yet."

Belle stood up and stepped away from the table, going to the door. She turned back to Addy and smiled brightly. "Thank you for today." She paused for a moment, her hand resting on the door frame. "Perhaps we could eat all of our meals together from now on?"

Belle had become so aware of her sudden change in attitude towards Addy. But the feelings she had towards her were not unpleasant, and so who was she to resist them?

Addy continued to hold that smile. "I would like that very much."

"Wonderful. Then, good night."

"Good night."

Chapter 14

A Feeling Like Roses
Adeline

The kitchen connected to the dining room through a hallway, and Addy walked in. Caris clocked her instantly, worriedly looking at her as she stopped washing some plates. Alvis and Wilmot stood further into the room, leaning against one of the work surfaces.

"Addy? What is it dear?" Caris asked, putting down a dishcloth. "You look terrified, what happened?"

Addy couldn't speak. Couldn't breathe. Her hands wouldn't stop shaking.

Alvis immediately pushed themselves off the counter and walked to Addy, putting a hand to her face. "You're burning up. Did she say something to you? I thought you two were having such a nice day together."

Addy shook her head. "No…" She mumbled. "No…she's…"

Caris put a hand on Alvis' arm, and they took a step back, dropping their hand. She tried to offer one of her signature comforting smiles. "Take a deep breath, dear. Then start from the beginning."

Addy inhaled sharply, completely covering her face with her hands. Through muffled words between her fingers, she spoke. "She's gorgeous."

"She's what?" Wilmot asked, now joining the other two spirits surrounding Addy.

Addy couldn't quite believe what she was saying. "She's gorgeous, and I'm screwed."

She dropped her hands. Caris looked over to Alvis and Wilmot. "Go find Belle, make sure she's alright, will you?"

"But…" Alvis started, but Caris cut them off.

"Don't make me repeat myself."

Wilmot and Alvis didn't protest further and left the kitchen.

Once the door was shut, Caris guided Addy to a wooden stool and sat her down.

"Now, tell me what happened in there."

Addy put her hands together, fidgeting with them as she tried to think of the words. "I'm starting to think of roses every time I look at her."

Caris frowned. "Roses?"

"You always told me I had an indescribable love for roses. It's the same when I look at her. I know we've only recently started to get along but now every time we talk, she reminds me of roses. And how I feel is so sudden but maybe I felt this way all along."

Caris took one of Addy's hands, holding it in her own.

"Dear, I don't understand what you're trying to say."

Addy could feel her throat tightening, and her breath hitch as she spoke. "Do you remember when you used to read me those stories about how girls would find a handsome prince and live happily ever after?"

"Yes, of course."

She squeezed Caris' hand tight as she continued. "And you always said afterwards that one day I could find a prince like that."

"Yes...I did."

"What if I didn't want that?"

As Addy looked up to Caris, she smiled. As she always did. Always willing to listen to Addy, and understand her. "Well, I can't force you to have something you don't want-,"

"What if I wanted a princess?"

As soon as Addy said those words, the world stopped spinning. Caris' white eyes glowed, processing what she had been told. It was the truth, pure and unfiltered. Now all that was left was the response.

Caris squeezed Addy's hand back. "I see nothing wrong with that."

Addy's face melted into a sob as Caris pulled her into a tight embrace. Caris rubbed her back, holding her as she cried. "There's nothing wrong with that at all."

*****

It took a while for Addy to calm down. When she had stopped crying, Caris made them both a cup of tea. She set the two cups down on the wooden work surface, and grabbed another stool, sitting next to Addy and taking her hand once more.

"So, you think that Belle is gorgeous?" Caris asked, giggling.

Addy rolled her eyes but smiled. "I think I've felt that way for a while but she hated me so harshly I couldn't think of her that way."

"Love is a curious thing." Caris used her free hand to reach for a sip from her cup.

Addy scoffed, still smiling as she took another sip of tea. "What should I do now?"

"In what sense?"

"About Belle, and how I feel. This is all so uncertain."

Caris put her cup back down on the work surface, and put a hand on Belle's arm. "There's nothing you have to do Addy. Despite my inexperience with something like this, I don't believe there's a certain set of rules you have to follow. Get to know Belle, now there is no fear between the two of you, and let whatever happens, happen."

"What if nothing happens?"

"Then at least have comfort in the knowledge you tried." She rubbed Addy's arm. "I have always told you to be kind. That dark spirit, all those years ago told you to have kindness in your heart. Extend that to Belle, and hopefully, she will start to see you as the person we see every day."

Addy nodded, finishing her drink and delicately putting the cup back on its saucer. "Are you going to tell Alvis and Wilmot about this?"

"Only if you want me to."

She shook her head. "Can we not tell them yet?"

"Of course. And if they try to ask you, you be strict with them. Or I'll be having words."

Addy laughed and reached for Caris' hand again. "Thank you, Caris."

Caris took it. "No need to thank me, dear."

Her smile faltered for a moment. "Do you think…if my mother was still around, she would be okay with who I am?"

Caris stood up from the stool and helped Addy to her feet."I think you should not spend your time worrying about events that will never happen, Addy."

"I know my parents are not coming back, Caris. I just…I would like to know how they would have felt. In moments like this. If everything was normal, how would moments like these go."

Caris put a hand on Addy's cheek, looking at her with a sweet smile. "I hope the moment would go exactly like this."

Addy pulled her in for another hug. Despite Caris' lack of solid form, there was still warmth in her hugs. She truly was like a second mother to Addy and surpassed her mother in every way. Caris took Addy by the arm and walked her back to her room.

On their way, they realised that night had fallen. There was no sign of Wilmot, Alvis, or Belle. When they reached Addy's room, she gave Caris one final hug before wishing her goodnight.

That night, Addy dreamt of nothing. But the feeling remained. The feeling of roses.

Chapter 15

Turn Back Time
Bellerose

"There's been a tunnel system in this castle the entire time I've been here?"

Belle and Addy were walking from the library together, having found each other there by chance. They had been making casual conversation as they walked towards the grand foyer, and when Addy brought up the castle's mysterious feature, Belle couldn't help but be interested.

"Yes, they've been here since the castle was built," Addy explained. "If you want, we can make a detour so you can see the one that leads to the garden?"

Belle agreed, and Addy turned a corner, leading Belle down a spiral staircase towards the back of the castle. They had to take the stairs slowly, with Addy sliding her hand across the stone wall and holding up the skirt of her dark green dress. At one point, Belle took her hand, stepping in front of her to lead her down. She used to be so scared of Addy's hands, but now as she took them, she knew there was nothing to fear any more. They reached the bottom of the stairs, and when Addy let go of her hand, Belle tried to ignore the burn she was feeling in her cheeks.

What was this feeling? And why did she feel it when she was with Addy?

"Here we are," Addy said, interrupting Belle's train of thought. She opened a beaten wooden door.

Belle looked inside and saw a completely dark tunnel. In the far distance, she could see a light leading back to outside. Next to the door, there was a table with an unlit candlestick.

"I wonder if this was where the witch ended up in that story I read." Belle wondered aloud.

Addy's head snapped to the side to look at her. There was a look of concern in her eyes. "W-what witch?"

"I found this book in the library, it looked like a diary of some sort but it seemed too fictional to be true. A witch ended up in some tunnels under a castle after stealing a mirror."

Addy's expression changed, but it was clear she wasn't going to tell Belle what she was thinking. But she was smiling, as if she was remembering an old friend. "When we are next in the library. can you show me that book?"

"Of course. But why?"

"Curiosity. It seems there is one book I haven't read yet."

Belle smirked, still wondering what was going through Addy's mind. All the same, she looked back into the tunnel.

"You are more than welcome to go through," Addy explained, as they both peered into the darkness. "I can't fit through them any more. They're human-sized, not beast sized."

Belle chuckled at the joke and looked at Addy. "Why were these even built in the first place?"

Addy paused, pursing her lips as she thought. "The castle was built from the riches my parents bargained with the spirits for. I think they had them built for when it was time to pay the debts."

She looked back at the tunnel, and back at Addy. It clicked into place. "You said you were the price of a debt. So if your parents made these tunnels to escape then..."

"They knew the spirit was coming back for them. They were told they would have to pay the price in ten years. They paid it on my tenth birthday, and that was only one debt."

"Is there a not a way for you to reverse this curse? Especially since it wasn't your debt to begin with."

"There is," Addy said after a moment of silence. Belle could feel her heartbeat quicken at the prospect of seeing Addy human again. "But it is an impossible task."

"How so? Maybe I can help while I'm here!"

Addy shook her head. Her tone of voice changed like she was somewhere else entirely. "It is nothing for you to concern yourself with. There is nothing we can do."

Belle sighed, ready to protest, but she knew that it was best not to push Addy further on this. She could tell she was already getting uncomfortable being here. Belle reached past Addy and closed the battered door.

"You don't want to go through?" Addy asked, raising her eyebrows.

"Not if I can't go through with you. But, thank you for showing me." Belle offered Addy her arm and gestured to the staircase. "Would you like to go get lunch together?"

Addy took her arm, and let Belle lead them towards the staircase. "I would like that very much."

*****

Night had fallen by the time Belle and Addy had made their way back to the library. When Belle opened the door and walked inside, she noticed there was already a small fire burning in the fireplace. The lamps on the wall were also lit, illuminating the bookcases surrounding them.

"Do you think your parents ever realised it was a little counter-intuitive to have a fireplace in a library?" Belle asked, turning around as Addy closed the door.

Addy laughed, walking to meet Belle in the centre of the room. "It probably never occurred to them, this room was always quite redundant. I think they had it made to show off they were not only powerful but intelligent too."

"Quite the performance," Belle commented with a small smile on her lips. She moved to the shelves, trying the find where she had spotted that diary Addy asked about. She scanned the shelves, but when she found the space on the shelf, the book wasn't there. There was an empty slot.

Belle looked over her shoulder and saw Addy standing behind her. She tapped on the wooden shelf. "It was right here! I put it back."

Addy narrowed her eyes, looking at the shelf. "Maybe Alvis took it?"

"Maybe, but that is still so strange…" Belle's voice trailed off and looked back at the shelf one more time. The rest of the shelf was undisturbed. As if the diary had vanished into thin air, or was never there in the first place.

She turned back around to see where Addy was, and found her at her usual reading spot, clearing some space. Belle shivered, the warmth of the fire not reaching her, and walked towards the fireplace. She stopped in front of it, holding out her hands to try and warm up her fingertips.

"Here."

She heard Addy's voice and looked up to see her unwrapped a blanket and gracefully draping it over Belle's shoulders. She held the ends in her claws, and at that moment their eyes met.

When Belle first saw Addy's eyes, she could only be fearful of them. But in the light of the fire, she realised they glowed like the sun. Everything about Addy looked different now, felt different now. She was not a scary monster wandering the forest, she was a marvel that stood the test and time and had weathered all storms. That was strong and mighty, but with a heart that still yearned for peace and love.

It was only when she let go of the blanket did Belle realise how pretty Addy looked.

"Thank you," Belle said, her voice only a whisper. Her cheeks burned again, but she could not tell if that was from the fire or Addy.

Addy seemed to pay no attention, sitting down on the window seat and making herself comfortable. Belle walked over, clutching the blanket tightly across her shoulders, and sat down on the other side, following the routine they had begun to have a few weeks ago. As Addy picked up her book and placed it in her lap, Belle looked out the window and gasped.

"What is it?" Addy asked, trying to see what Belle saw.

She pointed out the window, and up into the night sky. "There are twice as many stars as usual."

Addy grinned, looking up at the stars as well. "Indeed there is. And it's a calm night too."

"I used to watch the stars a lot from the front of our house. Once everyone had gone to bed and I had finished cleaning up. I enjoyed the quiet, for the brief moment it lasted. But with it came an emptiness."

"It's always been too quiet here. The spirits sometimes bring life but when they're not around...it's the same feeling."

Belle reached for Addy's hand, which was resting on top of the book pages Their fingers intertwined, the rough bark on Addy's skin scratching Belle's palms. She still held on.

"I wish I had acted differently. So that neither of us felt that way here."

Addy smiled at her and looked back out the window. "Well, we cannot change time, only move with it. And tonight, as you said, there are twice as many stars as usual. Let's enjoy the quiet together."

Belle slowly let go of Addy's hand and reached for her book. In silence, they sat and read until the night grew long and the call to sleep grew louder. But the silence was never empty. Accompanied by the stars, the two spent the night in peaceful company, together.

Chapter 16

Lasting Impressions
Adeline

Time passed. Time, among many things, is a currency that can be spent well if spent right. And time is what Belle and Addy thankfully had. With each passing day, the two of them found themselves drawn to each other's company, even if it wasn't planned. There were encounters in the library, walks through the garden, and conversations that ranged between the mundane and the exciting.

Addy realised how limited she was from being confined to the castle. Belle had perspectives she would have never thought about. Sure, she had heard plenty of stories from the spirits, but none were the same as Belle's. She brought an entirely new light to things. And over the passing time,

Addy noticed how Belle's reactions to her changed. There was no longer the sudden fear or horror when they saw each other. Less hesitation in her words. Thankfully, all preconceived ideas or prejudices were long gone between them.

On one of the many days when they spent time together, Addy was walking Belle through the castle. Lively chatter filled the air until Addy stopped in front of a set of double doors. She turned on the spot, trying to remember where she could take her next.

Belle looked over at the doors, raising an eyebrow curiously. "That's where the ballroom is, right?"

Addy stopped in her train of thought, following Belle's eyes to the doors. She hadn't thought about that room in years.

"Yes, but we don't use it."

Belle looked over her should to Addy. "Can we take a look inside? I've never actually seen a ballroom before."

Addy chuckled in response, disbelief in her voice. "You haven't been snooping around when we are not looking?"

She shook her head. "I was scared, and I did want to somewhat respect your privacy."

Addy stepped forward, twisted the door handle and pushed it open. "In that case, we can have a look."

The door creaked open, weary from years of not being used. Immediately, Addy could feel the change in the air, and it made her cough. There was no dust since she knew the castle would keep the room clean at least, but there was a stillness from nothing entering the room for over a decade.

Addy hadn't been here since her tenth birthday. But, the room hadn't changed one bit.

It was still golden. Gold; a design choice her parents adored. The round room was lined with gold columns. A gold chandelier hung from the ceiling. Along the back of the room, were gold-framed windows, leading out onto a long balcony. Gold and white marble floor.

Gold. Gold. Gold.

Addy had always wondered if it was ever real gold.

There was a raised platform where the orchestra used to play, but now there was only a piano covered by a white sheet. Belle walked to the middle of the ballroom, mouth hung open in awe at what she was seeing.

"My goodness, this is extravagant." She announced, her voice echoing off the walls.

"You're telling me." Addy joined her in the centre. "I forgot how...*gold* this room was."

"How long has it been since you stepped in here?"

Addy put her hands together. "The last time was the day I was cursed."

Belle spun around to face her, the pieces falling into place as she connected Addy's story. "You should have said, we didn't have to come in here."

She sighed, shrugging her shoulders. What was the point of keeping secrets from her any more? "It's alright."

Belle took a deep breath. It was obvious as she paused that she was trying to think of a direction to steer the conversation. "Do you know my father taught me to dance?"

Addy smiled, indulging Belle in her choice of conversation. "Oh, he did?"

"Yes!" Belle exclaimed, putting her hands out with a flourish. "He taught all of us, even my brothers. He said it was a great way to make an impression on someone."

"I see."

Belle held out a hand to Addy. "Have you danced before?"

The question surprised her. "Not since I was young, and I only used to mess around."

Belle seemed to understand, but her hand remained outstretched. "Can I try and teach you?"

Addy's smile shifted into a smirk. "Belle, are you trying to make an impression on me?"

Belle's face flushed. "M-maybe."

Addy took her hand.

"It's working," Addy smirked. "You lead, I follow."

Her face was still burning, as Belle realised something. "Wait one minute."

She bent down, knocking on the marble floor three times. Belle flinched, and Addy knew the castle's voice had entered her head. She kept a tight hold on her hand.

"Can we have some music, please?"

There was silence.

"No need to be in a mood, I said please."

Addy smiled, seeing Belle relax as the castle exited her mind. Not a moment later, as if out of nowhere, both of them heard the light sounds of string and piano. A piece perfect for slow ballroom dancing.

Belle took Addy's other hand, placing it on her shoulder. She put her hand on Addy's waist and kept hold of the other.

Addy felt like her heart was going to implode, and it seemed Belle felt the same. There was a tremble in her voice as she spoke.

"Alright, it's three counts, and then a pause. One two three and one two three."

Addy nodded. Belle led the dance, slowing down the counts to allow Addy time to move along. They were significantly out of time with the music, but there was nobody around to care. Belle lifted her arm to allow Addy to twirl, even as she stumbled out of it. Addy did the same, and Belle ducked under the tree branch that was her arm, spinning out to the side. The music seemed to realise what was happening, and changed, following the rhythm of the two of them.

Every step was reflected in the shining marble floor, their figures illuminated by the ludicrous amounts of gold that surrounded them. As the music went on, the two were moving as one, with Addy still counting the steps in her head as both of their dark blue dress skirts spun around.

This was the memory she wanted the ballroom to be associated with. Not anything else that came before.

Addy was out of breath and slowed down. The music came to a gradual stop, and Belle lead them both to the raised bandstand, where they sat on the edge.

"Not bad for your first attempt," Belle commented.

Addy's hair had come undone from every twirl, and she raised her hands to fix it. She laughed, blowing a strand of hair away from her eyes. "If I had proper legs, I would have proper rhythm."

Belle noticed Addy trying to move her hair. She shuffled closer, holding her hands out. "Here, let me braid it again."

Addy remained still as she got to work. Belle delicately moved Addy's hair around her horns and began to braid it.

"Did your father ever teach you to dance?" She asked.

"No, he didn't."

Belle leaned forward once she had finished doing Addy's hair. "I'm sorry, about what happened with your parents."

"Don't be. I found out after they were gone that they weren't kind people."

Belle put a hand on Addy's arm, saying nothing.

"Do you miss your family?" Addy asked, turning herself around to fully face Belle. "I know we've talked about them a bit but it has been a year since you came here."

Belle took a moment to answer. "Yes and no. I miss them, as anyone would miss their family. But, I am happy here, too. I've never felt more free in my life."

"Despite being stuck in a castle?"

Belle laughed. "Yes, despite being stuck in a castle. It's like what we said before, there were expectations and standards for what I needed to be that I would never have met. And, I suppose my family is not the kindest either."

Addy nodded in understanding. "There's something Alvis once told me. Blood is messy, and the water's clean. Sometimes the better family is the one you choose."

"I am glad I am here with you all." Belle moved her hand down to take Addy's, squeezing it. "I do still love them, though. And I wish I could see them. My sisters were engaged when I left. It would be nice to see if they are now married."

Addy let go of Belle's hands and quickly got to her feet. "There might be a way you can."

Belle stood up as well. "What do you mean, Addy?"

"Follow me. I'll explain on the way."

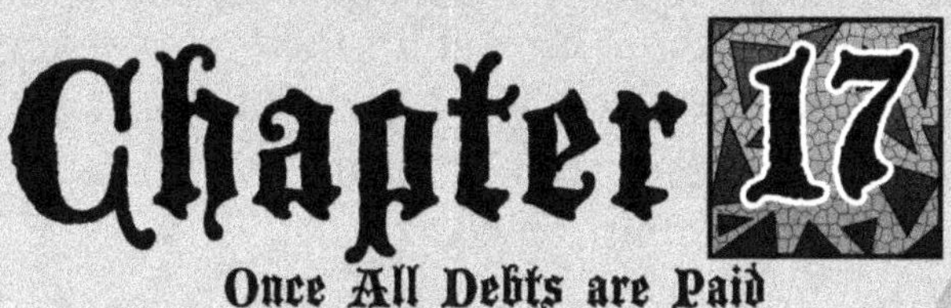 Chapter 17

Once All Debts are Paid

Bellerose

"I had completely forgotten about it until you talked about seeing your family."

Addy had led Belle up to her private quarters, pushing open her bedroom door. She began rummaging through the drawers, looking for something. Belle looked around Addy's room, noticing the scratches on the walls and the bedposts. The bed sheets were somewhat neat, clearly done by Caris to try and neaten up the room a bit. A stack of books from the library sat on the bedside.

"Here!" Addy announced with triumph, pulling out an ornate golden mirror. She handed it to Belle. "I found it a few years ago. I think it was left for me by...someone. I have my theories as to who but...well never mind that. It shows you who you want to see if you ask it."

Belle took the mirror from Addy's hands. "Really?"

"I think so. I did try to see my parents but that went as well as you would expect. But, try it! It might show you your family."

Addy looked over Belle's shoulder as she held the mirror in both hands. She spoke clearly to the looking glass. "Show me my family in Reverie."

The mirror shimmered.

There, inside the boutique in Reverie, were her father, brothers and sisters. Mira and Clara stood in front of mirrors, trying on wedding dresses, with the rest of the family looking on proudly.

Belle felt like she could melt as relief washed over her. They were okay.

"Oh, my sisters are trying on dresses." Belle almost laughed as tears form in her eyes. "Of course, they would go for the biggest ones."

Addy glanced over into the mirror. "Your family look so much like you."

"I'm the youngest." She pointed to her brothers in the mirror. "That's Eder and Faron. They're twins." She then pointed to Mira and Clara. "That's Mirabelle, and that's Clarabelle. I think my parents ran out of names to put before Belle, so that's how I became Bellerose."

"I can see the family resemblance," Addy replied, with a chuckle. She put a hand on Belle's arm. "You can keep the mirror if you want. I'm sorry I forgot about it until now."

Belle nodded, wiping her cheeks from the tears. "It's alright. Maybe I can use this to watch the wedding! I can see them walk down the aisle-,"

She was cut off by a familiar feeling. What was strange though, was that Addy seemed to react as well.

They both heard the same voice in their head at the same time. And the clatter of something falling to the floor.

Look down.

Belle slowly tilted her head to the floor, noticing a golden ring laying on the ground at Addy and Belle's feet. She bent down to pick it up.

Spin it three times, and you will be home. The debt of Marius Wood is paid.

The castle's voice vanished. For a second, neither of them could react, looking down at the ring in Belle's hand.

"I can go home," Belle whispered, her words sounding false.

Addy put her hands on Belle's arms. "Belle...this is wonderful news! The debt is paid! You can go to the wedding, see your family, go see the world like we talked about!"

Belle closed her fist around the ring and held it to her chest. Addy's excitement faded. "What's wrong?"

She was quiet. Because Belle realised what going home would mean. It would mean saying goodbye. "I would have to leave here. And leave you, and everyone, can't you come back with me?"

Addy's face fell, and she continued to keep her arms on Belle. "Oh, Belle. I can't. You know I can't, the curse binds me to this castle. That ring means your debt is paid. By giving you that ring the castle accepts your time here as payment. You need to go home."

Belle realised she didn't want to leave forever. As much as she wanted to see her sisters wed, she had come to see this place as her home. More of a home than Reverie ever was.

"If you asked me to stay, I would."

"I can't ask that of you. You can't remain trapped here with me. This is your chance of freedom Belle and I want you to take it. You need to take it and never look back."

Belle stepped out of Addy's embrace but took her hand. "I don't want to leave without you. Can I pay your debt? What's the price?"

Addy shook her head. "You know it's not my debt Belle, and it's a price neither of us can pay."

Belle's eyes went crystal as more tears formed. Addy realised she was crying too. "Please Belle, go. Go see Mira and Clara married, go do everything we talked about. Go, for me and all debts are paid."

She spoke with defeat as tears ran down Belle's face.

"There's no other way?"

"No. You need to go."

There must be another way. Another way to solve this. To pay all debts, to help Addy. She couldn't be left behind, Belle wouldn't allow it.

"I'll come back, and we'll find a way to pay the debt."

Addy averted Belle's gaze, sighing in disbelief. "There's no need. There's nothing you can do. Please, Belle. Don't fight with me. I do not want our last memory of each other to be a negative one."

Belle let out a long sigh and put the mirror back down on the dressing table. When she turned back, before

Addy could say anything, she pulled her into a tight embrace.

Addy inhaled sharply in surprise, before bringing her arms around and holding Belle close.

Belle realised she didn't want to let go. She didn't want to leave. But she knew she had to, she knew this was the price she paid. She kept telling herself in this quiet moment that she could come back once all debts were paid, but deep down, she knew this wasn't true.

Addy pulled away first. "Go get ready. Before the castle changes its mind."

*****

Belle was in her bedroom, gathering her things. She found the old dress that she wore when she first arrived, the light blue colour looking foreign to her now. She got changed and noticed along the skirt the stitches she had done to repair it a few months ago. There were also new stitches, from when she taught Addy how to fix the holes the had made in her dresses.

There was a knock at the door, and Belle hoped it was Addy. But, it was Alvis' head that appeared through the door. Belle smiled at the sight of their head levitating through the wood. "I still have not got used to that."

Alvis' stepped through the door, appearing fully. "At least that's one thing you'll miss when you're home."

Belle froze at their words and turned around. "Addy told you?"

They nodded. "She told us. While I am happy to see your debt paid, I am sad to see you go."

She smiled, swallowing back the tears she had only just stopped shedding. "I am sad to go as well."

"That's strange, considering how you were when you first arrived. So scared, so judgemental. I am glad I got to see the person you are underneath all of the performance."

Belle nodded, taking her blanket off the bed and beginning to fold it. "Did you need something, Alvis?"

"Yes." They stepped back out the door, and came back in, using the doorknob. They walked back over, handing Belle a small pile of books. "The ones you were going to read next. You don't have to worry about returning them."

Belle chuckled, holding the books to her chest and putting them in her bag. "Thank you, Alvis. I'll be sure to enjoy them."

Alvis paused before taking a seat on the edge of the bed. "You will make sure you take care of yourself when you're home?"

She still kept her smile but tilted her head towards him. "Of course, why wouldn't I?"

"You've grown a lot Miss Belle, I would hate to see that reversed."

"I promise, I will not forget any of this any time soon."

"If I had told you this when you were first here, you would have wanted to forget about your time in the castle. With the beast."

Belle felt her stomach knot, remembering her words to Addy back then. "Maybe. But now I can't imagine ever forgetting Addy."

"Good." Alvis gave her a gentle smile. "I don't think Addy can forget about you either."

At this, Belle blushed, making Alvis laugh. They made their way back to the door and turned around to look at Belle. "I hope no matter what comes next for you, you remember to follow your heart. Know yourself, and know yourself well and true."

"I will. Thank you for everything, Alvis."

They nodded and disappeared outside the door. Belle double-checked her satchel one last time before putting the books inside. That was everything.

But before she went to the door, she knocked on the bedroom wall three times.

I am sad to see you go, Belle.

"I never expected you to be sentimental."

I have gotten used to your company. Do you need something?

Belle frowned. "There is no other way, is there? I have to leave."

Your family's debts are paid. You cannot stay here, that is Addy's price. It is no longer yours.

"Can't I make a deal?" She asked suddenly. "Pay a price for Addy's freedom?"

It is not your debt, nor is it Addy's. Neither of you have any control over this.

"I see."

I feel your pain, Belle. You will be missed.

"Take care of her for me."

Of course. Oh, one more thing.

"Hm?"

I'm sorry for almost killing you with that plant.

Despite everything, Belle laughed out loud. "All is forgiven." She said, with a soft fondness, and the castle exited her mind for the final time.

Now, it was truly time to leave.

*****

In the castle foyer, one year after Belle had first arrived, she stood in front of Addy. The gold ring was now on her index finger.

Caris, Wilmot, and Alvis had gathered around the two of them. When Belle had left to get the blue cloak she arrived in, Addy had relayed the news to the spirits, who were all sad to see her go.

Caris pulled her into a tight hug first, which felt strange as Belle put her arms around her. "Take care of

170

yourself, dear." She explained, rubbing Belle's back. "And your family. Give yourself the life you deserve."

As they parted, Caris whispered one final bit of advice into her ear. "And remember to be kind to all you meet."

Wilmot was next, not offering a hug but instead a firm handshake. "Be careful as you go, Miss Belle. Weddings can be especially dangerous."

Caris nudged him. "Don't be silly, Wil."

"What? They can be! All that dancing can cause injury."

Alvis offered neither a hug nor a handshake but smiled. "Enjoy the books, Miss Belle."

Then, at last, it was Addy's turn to say goodbye. Belle immediately pulled her in for a hug, not caring that the spirits were watching. The two held each other for a long time. As Belle took a long deep breath in, she realised Addy smelt of roses. The same as the ones in the garden she grew. It was clear Addy was trying to not hurt her by holding her too tight. They parted, and Addy took Belle's hand in both of hers.

"I'll miss you. But go live, for both of us."

Belle smiled, her heart completely shattering. "I promise."

She stepped back, and Addy's hand fell. She touched the ring and spun it around her finger three times.

The world went black.

When Belle opened her eyes, she found herself at the town entrance of Reverie.

She found herself home.

Chapter 18

Let the Grief Kill You
Adeline

"You should have told her."

Alvis' words cut through the silence that was left once Belle had disappeared. Addy, feeling a wave of exhaustion wash over her, walked over to the stairs and sat on the step. Everything felt empty, and her mind was hollow.

"Told her what?" Addy asked, looking over at Alvis.

"You know exactly what I'm talking about Addy," Alvis said, their voice surprisingly hostile.

Caris stepped towards Alvis, putting a hand up to them. "Whatever point you're making, now is not the time."

She shook her head. "It's fine Caris. Yes, Alvis, I like Belle."

Wilmot looked confused. "Well, yes Belle seems to be a good person. I think we had all grown to like her."

"No, Wil. I like Belle. In the way that I would like a boy."

His eyes widened. "*OH*." Wilmot turned to Alvis, leaning towards them. "I still don't get it?"

Alvis looked at him, frowning. "She likes girls, Wil."

If Wilmot could look flushed, he would be in this moment. He pushed his shoulders back, fidgeting in his refined position. "Well I like girls too, what's the point you're making?"

"She wants to marry a girl."

"*OH.*"

"Why didn't you tell her you loved her?" Alvis asked again, taking a seat next to her and ignoring Wilmot.

"She was already upset about leaving. It would have made her even more conflicted, or pressured to stay. She might not have even felt that way about me. It was better to say nothing."

"Well, I'm not an expert on romance, but it seemed to me like Miss Belle did love you," Wilmot added, leaning against the stair rail. "I wish you would have taken that chance, Adeline."

Addy scoffed, and Caris put a hand up to Wilmot. "Do not make her feel worse about this." She sat down on the other side of Addy, putting an arm around her. "You let her go because you loved her, didn't you?"

She sighed, leaning into Caris' embrace a little, still aware of her horns getting in the way. "No curse could stop me from loving her. But she'll be free, and I'll die in that comfort."

"Wait, die?!" Wilmot sputtered. "What do you mean die?"

Alvis knew exactly what she meant. "It's the curse, remember? Do not let that love leave, or the grief will kill you."

Addy nodded slowly. Caris lifted her arm away, putting her hands to Addy's face. "Oh, Addy, you knew didn't you?"

"I knew. But it would have been selfish of me to ask Belle to pay another price."

"But…" Wilmot looked to the castle doors. "She said she would come back."

"I'll be dead before she does. When she does come back, the money my parents hid away goes to her. So she can travel."

"Are you sure?" Alvis asked.

"It's not like any of us can use it. And I doubt my parents will make a triumphant return."

Addy leaned down and knocked on the steps three times.

I am sorry for your loss, your majesty.

"Sure you are."

I mean it. I can see you are hurting. How can I assist?

"You heard what I said, correct?"

It all goes to Bellerose Wood.

"Precisely."

The voice of the castle disappeared. Addy went to get up. Caris and Alvis immediately took an arm each.

She put her hands together. "Right, the least I can do is try and get my affairs in order before the curse claims me."

Addy looked to the three spirits. Her friends, her family for all these years. They all look terrified. "I don't want any of you to worry. We knew this might happen, just as we knew I might spend the rest of my life like this. I stand by my decision, but I understand it is hard for all of you. If you want to leave now so you don't have to see my passing, I permit you to do so. But if you do decide to stay, then I will be forever thankful I don't have to die alone."

Caris took her hand, as white tears fell from her eyes. "I would never leave you, dear. You know that."

Alvis put a hand on her arm, their voice trembling. "And we would never let you die alone."

Wilmot stepped in front of Adeline and bowed low from his waist. He put a hand on his chest. "You spoke like the Queen you are, Adeline. We vow to be with you until the end."

Addy choked back tears, trying to keep her composure. She didn't want to admit it, but she was scared too. "Then, let's get to work."

*****

The spirits had not wanted to leave her side as they finished packing up the final rooms. It was a joint effort to throw the dust sheets over everything and tidy up the remnants of food in the kitchen and clothes in the wardrobe. As the days went on, Addy could feel the curse beginning to take a toll on her body. She was slower, weaker, and every movement took more and more effort.

Once everything was packed up, and Addy had signed the will documents Alvis had drafted, Caris brought her back up to her room. They embraced for a long time before Caris finally bid her good night.

When she was fully alone, Addy grabbed the golden mirror from her dressing table. She held it up to her face, ignoring the light fading from her eyes.

"Show me Bellerose Wood." She asked, in a quiet voice. The mirror shimmered and showed Belle in a village, which Addy realised was her hometown of Reverie. She was sitting on the front step, looking up at the night sky. Belle had described her house many times to Addy, and so she could recognise it through the mirror glass.

She was safe.

She was home. She would live.

Addy put the mirror down. She hoped that Belle would forget about her, and go on to live a long life, in any way she wanted to live it. Even though Addy would not forget about her.

She liked the fact, despite her circumstances, she had the memories of this last year fresh in her mind. They would be the last things she would remember when she closed her eyes one last time, hopefully in the rose garden.

At least she would die happy.

Chapter 19

Bellerose

Belle walked up to the front door of her family home in Reverie. The town had not changed in a year, but she had returned quite different indeed. She kept the books Alvis had given her clutched to her chest. In hindsight, she wished she asked Addy if she could have kept the mirror.

But maybe that was intentional. It had already broken Belle to have to leave Addy and return home. Maybe by not having the mirror, she was saving herself more heartbreak.
Belle took a deep breath and knocked on the front door.

The door opened.

Belle's father gasped and immediately pulled Belle into his arms.

The books fell out of Belle's hand as she was embraced by her father, who kept muttering her name over and over. He put his hands to her face, tears rolling from his eyes. Belle began crying too.

"Oh, my Belle! I am so glad to see you."

Belle put her hands over her father's, smiling at him. "It is good to see you too."

He let go of her face, took her hands and began to pull her inside. "Am I dreaming this? Is the debt paid?"

Belle resisted her father's pulling, bending down to pick up the books. She joined him at the dining table. "Yes, the debt is paid." She explained, in a quiet voice.

Her father sat down at the table. Belle put the books down and sat on the empty chair next to him, taking off her bag.

He took her hand again, running his rough fingers over hers. "And after only a year, the spirits must have been kind to you."

"They were more than kind." She looked around, noticing the rest of the house was empty. "Where is everyone?"

"Eder and Faron have gone hunting. Mira and Clara are overseeing the final touches for their wedding."

"Yes, the weddings!" Belle exclaimed, remembering what she saw in the mirror. "Of course. When are they getting married?"

"In a month. Everyone should be home any moment now. Oh, they'll be so happy you're home."

That moment arrived. Belle and her father had been talking casually about all the events she had missed while she was gone. Then, the door opened, and all of her siblings conveniently arrived at the same time. The reaction was first of bewilderment, but it turned to euphoria as each sibling embraced Belle. The family had once again gathered around the table, as they had always done.

Eder and Faron had not changed much, though Eder was now attempting to grow facial hair. The two of them still brought mud in from their boots and hazardously hung up their dirty jackets. Mira and Clara seemed to have become more refined since becoming engaging. The two now wore dresses with more finery on them, more silk ribbons and lace. Faron took charge of the conversation, catching Belle up on the conversations she had missed out on.

"It was tragic when Mira and Clara realised they would have to wash their dresses," Faron explained, slapping his knee as he laughed.

Mira scoffed, holding out a delicate hand. The one with her engagement ring on. "You were cleaning your clothes, you could have done ours as well."

"No chance!" Eder added, joining in on his brother's laughter. "I'm sure if you ask Belle nicely she'll start doing it for you again."

Clara tutted, glancing at Belle. "Somebody has to do it. We're both terrible at the job."

Their father stood up, walked over to the stove and grabbed the kettle. "I'll make us all some tea. I was telling Belle about the wedding before you arrived."

"Yes! The wedding." Belle leaned forward excitedly from her seat, resting her elbows on the table. "Tell me everything. I want to know all the details."

Belle was surprised by her sister's reactions. Mira and Clara looked at each other, then over to their father. Mira frowned. "Father, you invited her to the wedding?"

He looked over his shoulder to his daughter. "Why of course! She's your sister. Now that she's home she should come to the wedding."

Her sisters looked back at Belle. Her smile shook slightly. "Is there something wrong?"

"Well...it's just that..."

Clara began to talk, but Faron cut in. "You left so suddenly, and we didn't tell anyone what was going on. So, people talked. They have their theories."

"It might be considered a bad omen if you were to come, that's all. We don't want you to be put off by the negative reaction you might receive." Mira added.

Belle's father gave everyone a cup of tea and sat back down with his own. "Now, now. I believe Belle when she says the debt was paid. There's nothing to worry about."

"I don't want our wedding to be overshadowed by this." Clara snapped, picking up her teacup.

"But..." Belle looked away from her sisters and reached for her cup. "Didn't you explain to them that I was paying your debt?"

The whole table was silent. Belle's head shot up, and she looked around at her family, trying to get a glimmer of a reaction. "You didn't tell everyone what happened?"

"It was easier not to," Faron admitted, holding his cup in both hands. "We didn't know how people would react if they knew father was involved. He could have lost his business, and Eder and I could have lost our work.

Mira and Clara could have had their engagements called off."

"So I was a scapegoat?"

Belle's father took her hand. "No, my dear. It wasn't like that."

"I paid your debt, father! Does that not matter?"

"Of course, of course, it does!" Her father clutched her hand. "I am grateful you did that, we all are. But we had to be careful what we said and how we said it. It was a small price to pay so that you had a home to return to."

Belle slowly put her cup down. She could tell her father was trying to twist this onto her, and that anger ate at her insides. She took a long, slow breath to calm herself. "I came home so I could come to the wedding. Ad- the master of the castle, helped arrange a way for me to get home after the debt was paid."

"The master?" Eder's eyes sparkled. "I'd like to give that old bastard a piece of my mind for tricking us into this debt."

"No," Belle argued through gritted teeth, her voice almost rising to a shout. "You will leave that castle alone. And the spirits, and its master. You do not go near there, none of you. Do you understand?"

Everyone nodded, but Mira scoffed. "Someone's in a mood. But fine, I'll talk to Piero tomorrow."

"And I'll talk to Adrian," Clara added in agreement.

Belle relaxed, noticing how tense she had gotten. "Thank you."

Faron and Eder stood up from the table. "We're going to meet some friends at the tavern."

Once the brothers had put their coats and shoes on, they each gave Belle another warm hug.

Faron kissed her forehead. "It is good to see you home sister."

The two left, the door closing behind them. Mira and Clara rose from the table, claiming they both wanted to get some beauty sleep. The bedroom door closed with a firm slam. Belle's father stood up and wandered over to inspect the pile of books Belle had brought with her. She held out a hand as he brushed a hand over the covers.

"Please be careful with them. They were gifts."

"Gifts?" Her father let out a laugh of disbelief. "You left with gifts?"

And many other things.

Belle nodded. "It was a parting gift from a kind spirit."

Her father shook his head, leaving the books and kissing Belle on the cheek. "I have missed you dearly. And I never forgot what you did for us."

"I would hope not," Belle mumbled, reaching into the cloth bag and pulling out the pink blanket.

Her father's mouth dropped open. "You had it this whole time?"

"It's...complicated." She explained, shrugging. "The spirits have a strange magic."

He shook his head. "It disappeared from your bed one day. We thought you must have taken it with you."

"I didn't. But the spirits-,"

"If they were kind to you, they must have wanted something from you."

"It wasn't like that!" Belle protested, putting the blanket down on the table and standing up. "I..." She hesitated but remembered what Addy said. How she explained her troubles to Belle, and the comfort of knowing that there was no rush to explain...anything. "I will talk about everything soon. But, not yet."

Her father's reaction worried her, as he remained almost neutral in it all. It seemed the year had changed him as well. He embraced her once more, wishing her goodnight. "Now everything can get back to normal. As it should have been."

They both knew that was a lie.

Her father retired into the other bedroom, closing the door quietly behind him. Belle leaned against the table, looking around at the familiar house that she once considered her home. She knew that her family would have been surprised to see her, but it was clear they had changed. She wasn't sure what it was, but the fact that they blamed her for the debt, and for everything else... worried her.

Belle looked at the gold ring, still on her index finger. She laughed to herself and twisted it three times.

Everything went black.

For a moment, Belle thought that maybe, just maybe, it would bring her back to the castle, and she would have found the perfect loophole to see her family, and Addy again.

But there was no such thing.

The ring made her appear at the town entrance.

Belle couldn't help but laugh again, finding the trick of the ring amusing. She walked home again. Went through the front door again, and gathered her things before going to bed.

She dreamt of roses.

*****

A month after her return, Belle had begun to settle back into the life she had left behind. Her sisters had been taking her along to all their appointments for the wedding, subtly dropping the news that she would not be a bridesmaid, but a guest, to avoid people gossiping during the ceremony.

Belle did try to protest, reminding them again that she came home just for the wedding, but neither Mira nor Clara wanted to hear it. They both asked Belle to play along to make their husbands-to-be happy. Her sisters tried to soften the deal by agreeing to get Belle a new dress for the wedding that would still match their colour scheme. It now hung in their bedroom ready for the big day, a simple lilac dress with a layered skirt. Belle's only requests were that some roses be embroidered in gold thread, to remind her of Addy.

She thought of Addy daily. Always wondering if she was safe. She had started to wear the golden ring around her neck on a chain, keeping it tucked inside her clothes.

Her father came in through the front door, as Belle sat at the dining room table making flower arrangements. Peonies, lilies and daisies covered the wooden surface, as well as sky blue ribbon. Her father chuckled as he saw the sight before him.

"Your sisters are truly keeping you busy, my dear."

Belle thought of Caris, who would probably have sat with her to help her make the bouquets. "I think now they've paraded me around town to prove I'm home safe, they're putting me to work." She said, laughing as she pulled another flower from the many different piles.

Her father pulled out one of the wooden chairs and sat down. He cleared some space on the table so he could put his hands on there. "And your brothers? Have they been helping as well?"

Belle nodded. "They've been escorting me to the fountain so I can wash my clothes."

"Good, good. Belle, have you thought about what you're going to do after the wedding?"

She put down the flowers she was working on. "What do you mean?"

"You do not have a job here any more, and probably won't get one any time soon with people being suspicious of your return. My point is, what are you going to do with your life?"

Belle paused, trying to discern what her father was saying. "I'm not too sure, to be honest Father. I've only just come home."

"Exactly, and now is the time to maybe think about finding someone to settle down with."

"Oh." She finally realised. "You want my wedding to be the next one."

"That's putting it a little blunt but...yes." He moved closer to her, shuffling his chair across the hard wooden floor and taking her hand. "There are no more debts to pay, Belle. You can truly start a life now."

She remembered Alvis' last piece of advice before she left. "What about your work? Why don't I come to work with you?"

Her father shook his head. "My work is not for someone like you."

That hurt Belle more than she wanted to admit. If Wilmot were here, he would have probably punched her father. She almost smiled at the thought.

"Belle?" Her father interrupted, leaning closer and squeezing her hand. "Do you want me to see if there might be a man willing to have your hand?"

She suddenly clocked on to what her father was trying to do, and snatched her hand away, going back to working on the bouquets. "Can we talk about it more after the wedding, please? Let's not overshadow Mira and Clara's big day. And besides, I need to finish these so the ceremony can be set up."

Her father nodded, and Belle could see the shame on his face. "Of course...of course. We'll speak again after the wedding."

*****

The night of the wedding, Belle watched from the back of the room as her father walked Mira and Clara down the aisle in their elegant ballgowns. Eder and Faron stood to the side in their light blue suits, smiling proudly. She felt disconnected from it all like she wasn't part of that intimate moment her family shared. But, she was still happy to see it. Especially when the whole room interrupted as the newly wedded couples shared a kiss, and paper confetti was thrown around the town square. The revelry began not long after, with couples beginning to dance as the band began to play. Belle's father pulled her in for a quick dance, before switching to Mira and Clara. She danced with Faron and Eder, but as it turned out, both of them had found a lucky lady who caught their eye. She released them, backing away to the edges of the party, going to the table of refreshments to grab a drink.

"Belle?"

She turned to the voice and saw a face she hadn't seen for a long time. It was Thomas, still as serene as ever. Her face lit up. "Thomas!" She exclaimed, stepping forward.

He pulled her in for a quick hug. "It's wonderful to see you." He said as he let her go. "I've been meaning to stop by, but I never had the time."

Belle chuckled. "It's quite alright, Mira and Clara have been dragging me everywhere for the past month anyway. How are you?"

"Good!" Thomas said, happily. "Very well. Um...I'm married."

Belle put a hand over her mouth, hiding her grin. "Really? Oh, that's wonderful. Who's the lucky lady?"

Thomas pointed out into the crowd of people dancing. His hand followed a young brunette, dancing with a few of the children. "There. That's Nadia."

"Nadia? Oh, she seems lovely."

"She is!" Thomas rubbed the back of his neck. "I'm very lucky."

Belle put a hand on his arm. "I'm glad you're happy."

"I never got to tell you this, because you had to leave but, I wanted to say thank you."

She raised an eyebrow. "What for?"

"I know I was pretty hung up on the fact you rejected me but I'm glad you did. Because Nadia makes me happy, and if not for you saying no to my proposal, I wouldn't have met her."

"I am still sorry about hurting you."

"Don't be," Thomas replied with a grin. "It was for the best. How about you? How have you been? You just up and left one day, people thought you had made a deal with a spirit, or worse.

"Ah…" Belle paused, looking up at Thomas. "It doesn't matter, it's sorted now."

"Oh. good!" Thomas said, returning to his chipper tune. "So…any luck on Bellerose Wood finding love?"

Belle laughed. "Not sure about love, but I did meet someone."

Thomas' eyes widened in surprise. "Tell me about him!"

"Her, actually." Belle's smile softened. "Her name is Addy."

"Addy?" He nodded slowly. "What's she like?"

"Oh! Um…she's smart and knows a lot about plants. We used to read together in the library and talk about travelling. Her eyes are this intense yellow and they sparkled whenever she would ramble about something."

Thomas turned his head to her, a smirk on his face. "I see."

She didn't seem to notice, continuing her ramble. Exactly as Addy would.

"She looks after this rose garden, and told me about secret tunnels. We danced together, well I taught her how to dance. Even though her voice is deep there's a softness to it and even though I hated her at first she still spoke to me in the same way. I had to leave her to come back here and I didn't want to go but she was so…so selfless and she told me to leave to give me my best chance at life. And sometimes at night I would see her in the firelight and think she was the most beautiful person I had ever seen and…and…"

Belle took a sharp breath. Just as everything fell into place. "And...and I think I love her."

Thomas' expression was full of light and joy. "You love her?"

"Yes. I do."

"Does she know you love her?"

"No."

Thomas put his hands on her shoulders. "Then you need to go to her."

"What?"

He shook her lightly. "Never thought I would say this, on your sisters' wedding night. But, go to her."

"I can't·" Belle looked around. "My family, they'll·,"

"I'll cover for you!"

She couldn't keep up with all the emotions she was feeling. "Are you sure?"

Thomas sighed happily. "You've found someone who can love you the way you deserve. So go!"

He let go of her, and Belle pulled him in for one last hug before gathering the skirt of her dress and beginning to run. She ran home, throwing off the fancy gold shoes she was wearing into the corner and shoving on her brown boots. As she turned back around to head to the door, Faron stood in the doorway and grabbed her with both arms.

"Belle? Where are you going?"

Belle wrestled her way out of his grip. "Shouldn't you be at the party?"

"Answer the question."

She shook her head. "I'm going back to the castle."

"What? But you said you paid the debt. What other reason do you have for going back?"

Belle pushed past her brother and started stomping down the path from the house. Faron ran after her, grabbing her shoulder to pull her back.

"There's something I need to do!" Belle yelled, exasperated. "I need to see someone."

"Belle, everything was finally going back to normal. You can't undo this now, everyone is trusting you again-,"

"You told everyone I ran off and let them make up insane theories!"

Faron let go of her shoulder. "There was more to it than that. You had already caused a ruckus by rejecting Thomas. It was easier to not tell the full story."

"You tried to make me feel guilty for doing the right thing!"

He scoffed. "Oh, so you liked abandoning your family for a year?"

"At least it was my choice, Faron! Like it was my choice to leave, it is my choice to leave again. So, if you'll excuse me, there's someone I need to see."

Faron stepped forward, grabbing her arm this time. "Belle, whoever you need to see, they're not worth it. They're not worth your life coming to a standstill again. Please, come back to the wedding. There's someone Father wants you to meet-,"

"You are all obsessed over making me decide my life before I've had time to think about it!" Belle screamed, trying to pull her arm away.

"You don't have time Belle! Your life isn't something you have complete control over, no matter how much you wish it to be so. We have to do what we must."

Belle finally managed to wrestle her way out of Faron's grip. She reached for the chain around her neck, ripping it off. She put the ring on her finger.

"This is my life, Faron! It has always been my life! And finally, I am going to make the right choice."

She twisted the ring three times.

Hearing her brother's protests, the world went black.

Belle ended up at the town entrance. She saw the forest in the distance, and she ran.

*****

Belle ran through the castle gates, barrelling down the path as loose stones flew off to the sides. She pushed open one of the two doors and stepped into the foyer, bellowing Addy's name at the top of her lungs. She felt her breath catch, as her lungs burned. But still, she continued shouting. She leaned against the wall, trying to gather her energy, and as she was about to start searching, Alvis appeared in front of her, looking shell-shocked.

"M-Miss Belle!"

"Where's Addy?"

Alvis' face was frozen in fear. "The rose garden. You need to go to the garden."

They instantly disappeared, and Belle began to run again until she found the entrance to the rose garden.

Her heart dropped into her stomach. The world stopped spinning. Addy was lying, still, with Caris holding her in her lap.

Caris' voice trembled when she looked up to see Belle. "Oh, dear."

"Addy?" Belle's voice cracked, and she rushed towards her body, falling to her knees. "What happened? She was fine when I left."

Wilmot was standing at the opposite end of the fountain, and Alvis reappeared beside him. Wilmot spoke with sadness. "It's the curse, Miss Belle."

"The curse?"

Caris stroked Addy's cheek. "She didn't want us to tell you."
She allowed Belle to hold Addy in her arms. Belle could feel Addy's breath slowing. Caris stepped away, joining Wilmot and Alvis. There were tears in all of their hollow eyes. Belle moved closer to the fountain, leaning against it.

"Addy?" She gently shook her. "Addy, please wake up."

She remained still.

"Addy?"

Her breathing stopped.

Chapter 20

Free

Adeline

Adeline Stone woke to cold fountain water being splashed on her face. Her eyes struggled to open. She thought she was dreaming when she saw Belle holding her in her arms. Perhaps the spirits were being kind in letting Belle be the last thing she saw before she died.

But she wasn't dead yet.

"Addy!" Belle exclaimed, pulling her in and embracing her.

Addy could feel herself dying, though. Every breath hurt, and every heartbeat was slower and slower. It was like ivy vines were tightening around her bones. Like rose thorns were poking her heart. She lifted a hand, trying to touch Belle's cheek.

Addy's voice was quiet as she spoke. "I don't understand...you came back?"

"I came back. I was always going to come back."

"Why?"

"Because I followed my heart and it led me back to you." Belle's tears fell onto Addy's face, and she had the most beautiful smile. "I love you, Addy."

Belle leaned forward and kissed her forehead.

Then there was a bright light.

Adeline Stone felt the light absorb her. She saw the same thorns that had once cursed her, crawling up her skin and enveloping her. The same process as before is now reversed.

Well, to an extent.

When Addy re-emerged, she felt so...different. Belle stared at her, and she heard Caris let out a loud sob, with Wilmot holding her close. She rushed to the fountain, staring down into the water.

She was human.

To an extent.

All cursed features were gone. Except for those two brown twirling horns. Her skin, as well, had traces of thorns, like they were tattooed onto her skin. Her brown hair fell down her face, and her green dress fell awkwardly off her shoulders, now much too big for her. Her yellow eyes were now the green of the forest and the trees.

"What happened?"

Addy turned back to Belle, kneeling next to her. Before she could reply, Alvis spoke in pure disbelief. "The curse is broken."

"How? You said you couldn't pay the price."

"Not fully." Addy took Belle's hands. "I made a deal to reverse some of the effects of the curse. With the same spirit that cursed me. She took pity on me and wanted to give me a chance. The deal was, I had to find love."

Belle hesitated, still taking it all in. "That was the price?"

Addy almost laughed. "Yes. I didn't want to tell you, you shouldn't have been pressured to feel anything you didn't want to feel. I didn't expect to fall in love with you. I was content to let you go."

She smiled at her, that brilliant smile of Belle's. "If I'd known we were on a time limit, I would have tried to be quicker at working out my feelings."

Addy pulled her closer, putting a hand to her face. "There is no better time than now."

There was a sudden chill in the wind. And a voice that Addy hadn't heard for ten years. "I couldn't have put it better myself."

She got to her feet, turning to face the dark spirit. The same one that cursed her, and pitied her. The one who came to collect the price from her parents. Addy looked around, seeing that the other spirits had retreated, and Belle had pushed herself up against the fountain, still on the ground.

"It's you," Addy said, regaining her balance.

The dark spirit smiled. "It's me. I believe congratulations are in order." They glanced at Belle. "A pleasure to make your acquaintance, Bellerose Wood."

Belle's chin dropped into a low nod. "A pleasure."

"I applaud the two of you, for finding what is often so hard to find. And for overcoming the hardships that presented themselves. I knew you could do it."

Addy looked over her shoulder at Belle, and then back to the dark spirit. "You knew exactly what was going to happen, didn't you? You knew that when the time came, I would not want a prince at all."

The dark spirit chuckled in amusement. "Sharp as ever, and always to the point. I see all, Adeline. We spirits see the past, present and future. We see the way the tides can change and which direction the wind will blow. I knew it was not right to send a prince your way, to force you to be someone you were not."

Addy sighed, crossing her arms. "So I was always going to break the curse?"

"We are knowledge never-ending. We are trust and worship. We are fate. One day somebody would arrive at the castle. It so happened that Belle chose to pay her father's debt, and as such your fates were intertwined. You may not have fallen in love at all. The castle would have given Belle the ring and she could have never come back. But she did."

Belle had gotten to her feet, and stood next to Addy, taking her hand. "Because I realised I loved her?"

"Exactly. We knew what could happen, but in a matter such as love...you two had to put in the effort. And now tomorrow this land will wake up and remember their Queen as if she had never left them. And you two have found what many spend their lives seeking."

Addy swallowed, holding back tears. "I never knew you had such faith in me."

"You are as bright as you were when we first met, Adeline. I am sorry I cannot fully reverse the curse.

While your parents remain hidden, their debts remain unpaid. But I did what I could with my power."

The dark spirit opened their arms, and Addy stepped into the embrace like she had done when she was a child. The spirit lifted her head and planted a kiss on her forehead.

"The debts of Adeline Stone are paid."

Addy felt like a weight had disappeared. The dark spirit smiled widely and continued. "The debt to the castle is fulfilled, but I leave it to you as a parting gift, so that it may continue to take care of you and Belle. The spirit of the castle told me it likes you both. I'm sure the spirits who have grown so fond of you would wish to stay with you as well."

The dark spirit put a hand on Addy's shoulder. "I continue to believe in you, Adeline. And you too, Bellerose. Good luck."

Then they vanished.

Chapter 21 

We Begin Again
Bellerose

As the spirit vanished, Addy turned back to Belle, and the two embraced. Alvis, Wilmot and Caris all reappeared, crying with delight and taking turns to make comments about Addy's return to being human.

"Oh, it's a miracle!" Caris cried, hugging Addy again, and then going to embrace Belle. "I knew you would come back, dear."

Alvis wiped their eyes with their hand. "Did not think I would be this emotional."

Wilmot nudged Alvis, letting out a roar of joyful laughter. "You were sobbing with the rest of us Al!"

"Hang on a moment." Belle stepped out of the group, putting her hands up. She looked to Addy, narrowing her eyes. "You're the *Queen*."

Addy shrugged. "By a technicality, yes."

"You're the Queen!"

"Again, technicality."

"Her parents made a debt to get the title," Wilmot explained.

"It's a complicated affair," Alvis added.

Belle put her hands on Addy's shoulders. "We've had a QUEEN this whole time!"

"You're really hung up on this," Addy said with a chuckle.

"Yes, I'm hung up on this! You're our Queen!" Belle exclaimed, still in shock. "This is huge!"

"Not really. I'm not the Queen of everything."

"What?" Belle lowered her hands, moving them down to Addy's arms. "What do you mean?"

Caris giggled. "Addy is royalty, but not the Queen of the whole land."

Addy moved Belle's hands away and sat her down on the fountain. "When my parents made a deal with the spirits to get royal titles, it turns out they weren't specific enough. I'm only Queen of this castle."

Belle sputtered out her next words. "Really?"

Alvis chuckled. "Yes, we checked the official documents her parents received. Turns out the dark spirit has a wicked sense of humour. The only land Addy is Queen of is the land owned by her family. So, the castle, the gardens, and a small part of the forest."

"You're kidding."

Addy shook her head, taking Belle's hand. "Nope."

Belle started laughing. "That's so stupid of your parents! So when the dark spirit said tomorrow they'll remember their Queen...?"

"They'll remember the Queen of a very small kingdom."

She couldn't stop laughing, leaning into Addy as she covered her mouth. However, the laughter was cut off, as the five of them heard shouting in the distance. Wilmot vanished and came back a moment later.

"Um... two young men are shouting at the castle gates. Demanding that we...*release* Belle."

Belle rolled her eyes. "For goodness sake. Hang on."

She knocked on the fountain three times.

Hello again.

"Would you kindly tell my brothers I'll be back in the morning?"

Gladly.

They remained in silence as the sounds of her brothers swearing and shouting echoed across the garden. Belle and Addy laughed again. Caris tapped Wilmot and Alvis on the shoulder, dropping her voice into a whisper. When they were finished conversing, she looked up to Addy and Belle.

"We're going to go back inside. And let you two talk privately."

The three spirits vanished. Thus, the two of them were now left alone.

Addy looked at Belle sheepishly, before realising the dress she was wearing. "You left your sisters' wedding to come see me."

Belle shrugged. "It went downhill quickly. I wasn't even a bridesmaid."

She laughed. "Oh, how terrible. Are you sure you don't need to back sooner?"

"They can wait until the morning."

There was a long pause, as Belle watched Addy awkwardly try to find the words to say. She looked back towards the castle, then back at Belle, her now human hands knotted together with nerves. "What do we do now?"

Belle carefully took Addy's hands in hers. "Tell me you love me."

For the first time, Belle saw Addy blush bright pink. "I love you."

"Ask me to stay with you."

Belle let Addy pull her closer. "Stay with me."

"Ask me if I can get used to the horns."

Addy chuckled, holding Belle in her arms. "Can you?"

Belle leaned in close. "I always thought they suited you."

The two kissed. And it was like the world began again. As if fate had led them to that moment, to that garden. To roses.

Adeline Stone's twenty-first birthday was not a disaster.

Thank goodness for that.

A year after her curse had broken, she was finally used to having a human body. Wilmot taught her to walk again and even began teaching her some basic sword fighting when she was interested in a lesson. Alvis was glad to no longer see rips and tears in the library inventory, though instead he now had to deal with tea stains and ink marks. Caris was the same as ever, still motherly, still affectionate, enjoying the life that had been brought into the home.
Barnaby, along with the other spirits, still came to tell stories. The spirits' happiness over having a second audience member was never-ending.

As for Belle, well it could not be more perfect.

Sure, there were some bumps along the way. They still had plenty to learn about each other. Many long discussions sometimes descended into disagreements, but they overcame them. The year they spent travelling together opened their eyes to exactly what the world was, and what their place was in it.

Belle's family were hesitant to accept the fact that their youngest daughter and sister had fallen in love with another woman, let alone someone who used to be a beast and whose appearance was now akin to the spirits of the forest. There was still some hostility, but Belle was determined to keep trying. Especially after Addy proposed on the beach, by the ocean.

However, Belle and Addy had accepted dinner at Thomas and Nadia's home, which had turned out to be a wonderful experience. A kindness they would often repay.

Addy stood in the middle of the ballroom, smoothing down the non-existent creases of her dark blue ballgown. She tugged on the long lacy sleeves and smoothed out her hair.

She had forsaken crowns, with Belle finding an alternative in weaving gold chains and black and blue jewels from Addy's horns.

Wilmot and Alvis were waiting by the piano. Caris appeared in front of Addy, putting her hands together.

"She's outside. She's nervous."

Addy chuckled. "Why is she nervous?"

"Because it's a new dress. Another option for the wedding."

"Ah." Addy gathered her skirt and walked forward to the door, putting her hand on it. "Belle?"

Belle's voice came through from the other side. "Sorry, I thought I was ready."

"It's okay. But *ma cherie*, I would like to dance with you please."

The door opened a crack, and Addy saw Belle's hand slip through. She took it. "I believe in you." She whispered.

Belle pushed open the door, and Addy was stunned by her.

A contrast to what she used to wear, Belle was dressed in a golden gown, with enough shimmer that she could outmatch the ballroom itself. The sleeves went off her shoulders, covered in small gems. Around her neck, she wore the golden ring, now on a new chain.
"What do you think?" She asked, nervously looking up at Addy.

Addy grabbed her hands and pulled her in. "You look perfect."

Belle kissed Addy on the lips, and they both heard Wilmot announce to the castle. "Music maestro!"

The two danced. The feeling of roses blossoming between them. Forever strong and true.

And true to themselves they were, when appearances cast shadows of doubt. For such a beauty and such a beast, found love where it was thought to have never been found.

The End

<u>Acknowledgements</u>

To my family, for their endless support and
encouragement.

To Sam, for being the best ally a sister could ask for.
Thank you for all the times you've supported this book.
And for all the times you maturely handled my reaction
to Luz and Amity in the Owl House. And Barney and
Logs in Dead End. And Amaya and Janai from the
Dragon Prince. And Troy and Benson from Kipo.
And...honestly Sam there have been a lot of times
where I've gotten excited over gay couples. Too many to
include in this acknowledgement. So...*puts my middle
finger up.* Love you.

To Wynn, for the absolute relentless support you have
towards my work.

To Dorian, for...everything really. If anyone wonders if I
had any real life inspiration for Addy and Belle, I'll
point them in the direction of you and James‚ so they
get a special mention as well.

To Jay, for the absolutely INCREDIBLE artwork you
saw at the end. Thank you for taking on my request,
and for also being an amazing friend.

To the rest of the House, for being my family across the
sea. I hope one day I can cross the ocean to meet you.

To Adam, Becky, Ben, Scarlett and Stu. I just think
you're all pretty neat.

To all my fellow LGBTQ+ friends, you are loved, you
are valid, and you are worthy of every joy life brings
you. Never give up.

When The Beast Met the Witch

She can stay a week, and then he will come to get her.

That is what Adeline Stone was told when I arrived at the castle in the woods. I admit, she took the whole thing rather well. Much better than any other person I've encountered. But then again, as I soon discovered, Addy is cursed to take on a beastly form and was raised by spirits since she was ten years old. So...a wandering witch arriving under her home was nothing completely out of the ordinary. Even though I did scream at the first sight of her.

It turns out that stealing a mirror is trickier than one would think. We both thought it would finally give me some leverage, a bargaining chip so I could once and for all be left alone. But it seemed I was wrong. As it turns out, he's still watching me, tracking my every step. I don't think he's ever going to let me go, and the thought of that terrifies me.

We didn't know he was checking the mirror dimensions. If we had known, I would be smashing every mirror I encountered on my travels. So for now, to throw him off the trail, I was sent here for a week, until we know it's safe for me to move on. The plan is to throw him off my trail by dropping me off somewhere he would think I would never go. A place with no thralls or adventure.

And it seems like the plan is working.

Addy is kind enough, and a gracious host. She is only a few years younger than me, but my is she curious. Our conversations are varied and vivid, she has a wealth of knowledge, and I am only too eager to exchange it.

Turns out, the spirits of this world like to visit her, and have heard of my name through their various communication channels. That seems to explain why the castle of all entities knew exactly who I was. Addy has asked me plenty of questions about where I've been, but sadly I have had to be deliberately vague on the details.

However, she did explain her curse to me, and about this world's rules regarding the spirits and the prices you pay when making a deal with them. About how every debt must be paid. An intricate system built on promises, and pinning value on human idiocy. Even though she did not say it out loud, it was clear to me that Addy's situation was not her fault.

I quite like her. Once the week is gone, part of me will miss this strange beast. Or human. I like to think she is both.

The week is almost up, and I've not heard from him. I'm hoping this is because he is making sure the trail of my path has gone cold. If anything did happen I would never forgive myself for it.

I think Addy could see my worry when we sat down for dinner one night. She pushed further than I might have preferred, but there was no reason to hide my worry when I knew I was safe.

What she said was strange, but somewhat reassuring. It turns out, when I arrived at the castle, I made a deal with it. The deal was I can stay for a week, and then he has to come to get me. The castle had given my companion a very strict deadline to retrieve me. Addy reassured me that, if my companion knew the spirits as well as she guessed he did, he would know better than to go back on his word.

So he will come for me. He must because he knows better than to break a promise.

The week is up, and right on cue, a portal opened in the room I was staying in, and I heard his voice.

'Sorry for the delay, I'm here now. We need to go.'

I admit, part of me wanted to take a moment to say goodbye to Addy, but I knew the castle would not want me to overstay my welcome.

We decided to leave Addy the mirror.

The mirror has power and allows you to see whoever you wish if only you ask it.

This world's spirits can bind it here, and contain it. That is a promise they have made to us, through their whispers in the forests and oceans. It will have to do, for now.

Onwards I go then, to paths I have not found yet, and worlds I have not seen.

To my newfound friend Adeline Stone,

I apologise for my sudden departure, but my time here is up and as you were told, he has come to get me.

I leave you with the mirror I stole. I promise no harm will come from it being in your position, so consider it a parting gift. I thank you and the spirits again for your kindness.

Simply tell the mirror who you wish to see, and it will show it to you. I'm sure you can find a use for it.

I hope one day we can meet again and under better circumstances.

Yours,
Lilith Drayke

<u>**About the Author**</u>

Emma (she/they) is an author, artist, jack of all trades and being of chaos. She is an absolute nerd (and proud of it).

Her published works are all independently produced. Yes, this means they are very tired.

When they're not writing, Emma is either in the theatre (both onstage and backstage) or in a cafe rolling a d20.

She can be found on Instagram, TikTok, Twitch Twitter and YouTube if you search "PixieStarr"

They are aware that they are talking in the third person, and will stop doing so now.